# A GIRL LIKE YOU

---

SAMANTHA CHASE

D1520684

Editor: Jillian Rivera

Cover Design: Uplifting Designs/Alyssa Garcia

1

"I'm in hell."

"Dramatic much?"

Sam Westbrook glared at his twin sister Mallory. "It's not dramatic. It's a fact."

Mallory rolled her eyes at him even as she smirked. "Care to clarify, then? Because from where I'm sitting, your life is pretty damn sweet."

Now it was his turn to roll his eyes. "Okay, if anyone needs to clarify anything, it's you. How could you *possibly* think my life is sweet? Look around, Mal! This is not my life! This is like some kind of nightmare!"

The look she gave him said it all – and yeah, he was being dramatic. Sam knew he was being unreasonable, but this *really* wasn't the life he wanted for himself. This was a life that had been forced on him and he was counting down the days until he was free to go back to the way things were. To the life he had made for himself.

A life *not* in Magnolia Sound.

Only two hundred and seventy days to go.

"Sam, you have to get over it and move on. If you

stopped being so angry, you'd see that your life here is really great. The business is doing well, the town is rebuilding which is helping the business grow, the work on the house is coming along and looking great, we're all together so you're surrounded by family..."

"Mal, I think you're listing the reasons why *your* life here is great," he grumbled.

Mallory stood and slapped him on the back of the head on her way to the refrigerator. Reaching in, she grabbed two bottles of water, handing Sam one. "Why are you fighting this so hard? You're making more money than you ever have, you're living rent-free, I mean...think about it! There are worse situations to find yourself in."

"Maybe."

"No, not maybe. Definitely!" She sat back down beside him at the kitchen table and smiled.

He couldn't remember the last time he felt like smiling.

Oh, wait, yes he could! It was almost six months ago – right before Hurricane Amelia ravaged the East Coast and destroyed not only a large portion of the small town of Magnolia Sound, but also their family. The storm may not have directly killed his great-grandfather, but the fact that their family patriarch perished during the storm didn't lessen the blow. When Ezekiel Coleman died, it left a big hole in all their lives. Within a week of his death, Sam found out his great-grandfather left him a landscaping business – the biggest one in Magnolia Sound. Most people thought it would be a dream come true for him, but they were wrong.

So very wrong.

Did Sam enjoy working with plants and trees and shrubs? Yes.

Did he love being outside and making his own hours? Yes.

Did he want to be stuck here in this small, hick town for the rest of his life? Hell no.

Growing up, he'd spent most of his summers here and developed a reputation for being a hell-raiser – and he was proud of it at the time. Now? Not so much. Unfortunately, no one around here seemed to forget anything and no matter where he went or what he was working on, there was always someone ready to remind him of all his past transgressions.

So much for people deserving a second chance.

Mallory placed her hand on his and it broke him out of his reverie. "I wish you would give this a chance."

"I have!" he said a little too loudly. "You know I have, but the good people of Magnolia don't seem to want to ever let me forget all the shit I pulled when I was just a kid!"

"Sam, it wasn't that long ago when you admitted you almost got caught peeing in the church parking lot!" she reminded him with a small laugh. "You were hardly a kid and you knew better!"

Okay, so maybe he hadn't been trying all *that* hard to morph into an upstanding citizen, but still...

"Whatever," he murmured, slouching in his seat and raking a hand through his hair in frustration. "All I know is I have nine months left before I have my freedom back. Then I'm free to sell the business and go and do my own thing."

"You know that would break Pops' heart."

Yeah, he knew that and he didn't particularly like it, but Sam was also a little pissed that Pops had put him in this position in the first place. Getting the inheritance wasn't a bad thing, but the stipulation that Sam stay in Magnolia and run the business for a full year was. And if Sam refused to follow those rules, he'd lose the business to his cousin Mason.

Unbelievable.

"He knew exactly what he was doing, Mal," Sam reasoned. "He knew he was forcing me to stay in one place and play by his rules – rules I was never very good at following. But I'm doing the right thing by him for the next nine months. After that, according to his will, I am free to do whatever I want with the business."

"I wish you'd reconsider."

"And I wish we weren't having this conversation, so..."

She let out a loud and overly dramatic sigh. "Want to come over for dinner tonight? I know Mom's going out with Colton, so if you don't want to be here alone you're more than welcome to join me and Jake. We're just grilling some steaks if you're interested. And it will be an early night since it's a Wednesday and Jake has to get up early for work tomorrow, so..."

And that was another reason Sam resented being here – everyone had a social life but him.

Correction – a *romantic* social life.

Since he'd never stuck around very long in the past, he was fine being a little of the love 'em and leave 'em type. Now that he was living here full-time? Uh, yeah...that wasn't going to work out too well for him and it certainly wasn't going to help his reputation.

Something he found out after the first month here.

How was he to know Rhonda and Kim were sisters? Yeah, that was an extremely awkward night and he'd been laying low ever since. Well, he'd been laying low here in town. He'd managed to convince his cousin Mason to drive down to Wilmington with him a couple of times so he could find someone to hook up with who he wasn't going to run into while out on his landscaping route.

It was exhausting and far too constricting of a lifestyle for him.

At first, he had seriously considered turning down the inheritance and just letting his cousin have it, but after he had calmed down, Sam knew that was the coward's way out. Like it or not, Pops wanted this for him and after all the ways Sam had rebelled and Pops had bailed him out, it was the least he could do.

No matter how much he resented it.

He had been given three months to get his stuff in order back in Virginia before he had to officially take the helm at Coleman Landscaping. Quitting his job hadn't bothered him – it was just one in a long line of jobs he'd had in the last several years that bored him – but it hadn't taken long for him to realize there wasn't much holding him to his life there either. Sure, he had buddies he hung out with, but saying goodbye to them – even temporarily – really didn't faze him all that much.

That wasn't normal, was it? Was he some sort of sociopath who didn't have any real feelings toward people? Or was it strange how he never developed any kind of attachment to a job or a place? Holy shit, what if something was seriously wrong with him? Did everyone else think this about him? Know this about him? Was he some sort of danger to society?

"Earth to Sam!"

Oh, right. He was in the middle of a conversation. Clearing his throat, he decided to get off the topic of himself and on to another awkward one. "Does it bother you that Mom is dating?" he asked his sister.

She shrugged. "It was a little weird at first, but...I don't know. This is the happiest I think I've ever seen her, and Colton is a really nice guy."

Sam couldn't disagree. "It's a little annoying how Mom's got a more active social life than I do."

"And whose fault is that?"

He shook his head and reached for his bottle of water. "This town's!"

"Oh, my gosh, are we back to that again? For the love of it, Sam, let it go! You did a lot of stupid things and now you have to prove to everyone that you've changed! It's not a big deal."

"Why should I have to?" he argued loudly. "I don't stand around passing judgment on everyone, so why do they get to do it to me?"

"Not everyone is..."

"Oh, please," he interrupted. "Everyone is so damn uptight around here it's almost painful."

"Not true," Mallory said with a soft sigh. "You are completely exaggerating and you know it."

Leaning forward, elbows on the table, Sam smirked. "Mal, you and I both know that no matter where I go, people give me looks." When she went to comment, he cut her off. "Old Mrs. Whitman at the grocery store? She always shakes her head and gives me a disapproving look when I go in there."

"You stayed out all night with her daughter Penny the summer we were seventeen!"

"She needs to move on! Penny's married with three kids!" Shaking his head, he continued. "Then there's Mr. Jenkins at the bank. I do all my personal and business banking there and he still acts like he doesn't want to touch my money."

"I'm sure you're imagining that," she began and then

her eyes went wide. "Oh, wait! You dated his daughter that same summer! When Penny was grounded, you took out *his* daughter! Her name was Jen or Jan or something like that."

Groaning, Sam hung his head.

"So the parents of this town aren't too fond of you. Some of them have good reason."

"It's not just the parents. That uptight librarian is always looking at me funny too. Like she peers at me over her glasses like she's disapproving of something."

"When do you go to the library?"

"I don't!" he cried. "But I take care of the property next to it and whenever she sees me out there, I get the over-the-glasses glare."

Mallory studied him for a moment. "Wait. You mean Shelby? You know she's..."

"Doesn't matter." He shrugged. "I don't know what her name is. All I know is she's definitely got some kind of stick up her butt about something."

"Sam, Shelby's our age. Are you sure you didn't hook up with her and never call her again?"

"Please, does she even look like my type?"

"Ugh...you are the worst. You know that, right?" she said with a hint of disgust. "It's amazing you even remember what some of these girls look like with how quickly you go through them."

"Dammit, Mal, it's not always that! I'm telling you, the people of this town are the worst!"

He knew his twin well enough to know she was carefully considering her words and mentally counting to ten before she spoke. After a minute, she looked at him serenely. "While I am sure there are some residents here in Magnolia who aren't particularly nice, I can't think of one who has gone out of their way to make a spectacle of themselves like you seem to thrive on doing."

"I haven't in a long time!"

"A long time? Really? Do you realize you're the reason there is a 'No Public Urination' sign next to the *church*? For crying out loud, Sam, Pastor Steve was devastated that he had to put it there!"

He didn't mean to snicker, but...it just sort of slipped out. When Mallory shot him a sour look, he instantly sobered. "Yeah, he's the worst for sitting and passing judgment and really, he shouldn't."

"Oh, this I've got to hear," she said, her voice dripping with sarcasm.

"As a pastor, isn't it his job to preach forgiveness and not judging others? Isn't that biblical or something?"

The look she gave him said she agreed with him, but he knew she wouldn't say it out loud.

"So he and his secretary..."

"His wife," Mallory corrected.

"Whatever. So he and his *wife* look at me with those pinched expressions like they're sucking on lemons or something, and yet he continues to call and ask for estimates on working on the church grounds." He paused and took a sip of water. "I mean, why? He clearly knows it was me so...is he just trying to bait me into coming to the church so he can yell at me? Condemn me? Pray for me?"

She rolled her eyes.

"If you were me, would you go there? Knowing how he felt about you?"

"For starters, I never would have done what you did."

Now it was Sam's turn to roll his eyes. "Yeah, yeah, yeah...you're perfect. Can we just *pretend* for a minute? Put yourself in my shoes?"

"Sam..." she whined.

"C'mon, Mal. Humor me."

She let out a long breath. "Okay, fine. No. I probably would not go there."

Her answer pleased him greatly.

"However..."

*So close...*

"You *could* send one of your top guys over to talk to Pastor Steve. You wouldn't have to do it yourself. It could be a good contract for you and good for the business. As a businessman, can you really afford to turn down jobs just because you're embarrassed by your previous behavior?"

And that was the thing with Mallory – she had a way of putting things into perspective that made complete sense so he couldn't argue with it. The work the church needed was fairly extensive. They were going to take down a bunch of trees and create a small park on the church property and wanted Sam to do all the landscaping – including designing the space.

Apparently, someone had let it be known that Sam had some skills in that department and now they were interested in having him design something custom for them.

*Ugh...why me?*

"I guess I'll think about it," he murmured.

Mallory sat up straighter and smiled. "Excellent!"

And now he just wanted to move on to another topic. "So what else is going on with you? Anything exciting?"

"Not really. Wedding plans are at a standstill until we can get the work done here. I'm too afraid to set a date and then risk having the house unfinished."

He laughed softly. His sister had a weird obsession with this house ever since they were little kids. It was their great-grandfather's home and it had been in the family for over a hundred years. While it was nice, he never felt the connection to it that Mallory did. With their mother inheriting it and deciding to turn it into a bed and breakfast, there were a ton of changes it was going through, and she still was mildly obsessed with it. "Your fiancé is the contractor for the entire job, Mal. Surely he knows when the house will be done."

"You would think," she muttered and instantly cleared her throat and put a smile back on her face. "Jake and the crew aren't the problem. Mom is."

"What?" he asked with a laugh. "How is that possible? She's been very hands-on with the whole thing and all she does is talk about the work that's going on and how happy she is!"

"Sure, she's happy, but she also keeps changing things! Half the original plans have been scrapped because she's come up with a better idea. She spends way too much time on Pinterest looking up design ideas and then not understanding why she can't implement them all. She's making Jake crazy and she's frustrating me because it's always been my dream to get married here. The longer she drags this out, the longer I have to wait!"

"Maybe that's her plan," he teased. "Maybe she's not really on board with you marrying the boy next door, ever think of that?"

Mallory's eyes went wide and she paled. "Do you...I mean...do you think that could be it? I always thought she was okay with me and Jake and our relationship. There was a time when it was a little awkward, but..."

Instantly, Sam felt bad for teasing her. Reaching out, he placed a reassuring hand on hers. "Mal, relax, I'm just messing with you. Mom adores Jake and we're all happy for the two of you. Seriously, I was just kidding around."

She practically sagged to the floor with relief. "Not funny, Sam!"

"Come on. It was a little bit funny."

She stuck her tongue out at him. "Not even a little bit. And just for that, I should invite Pastor Steve over for dinner to talk to you tonight!"

"You wouldn't dare!" But he saw the twinkle in her eye and knew she was just trying to get even. His sister was many things, but she wasn't mean or spiteful.

She was the angel to his devil.

"You're right," she said with a pout, "but I really wish I could!"

"Nah, you're too nice." He took another drink of water. "So what else has Mom changed?"

Standing, Mallory waved him off. "We'll talk about it tonight over dinner. Be over at seven and bring some wine."

If a bottle of wine was all it was going to take to get a free dinner, Sam was completely on board.

---

"I think I'm in a rut."

"No kidding."

Shelby Abbott rested her face in her hands and sighed. "No need to agree so quickly."

"Shell, I'm not trying to offend you..."

"Could've fooled me." Okay, she was being a little bit of a drama queen right now, but when your best friend basically agreed with how pathetic your life was, it didn't quite inspire warm, fuzzy feelings. Tilting her head, she looked over at the one person who knew her better than anyone. "So what do I do, Laney? I am desperate for something...

something exciting to happen to me! Something! Anything!"

It was late Friday afternoon and they were sitting in the breakroom in the library. Their shifts were over, but instead of simply collecting their things and leaving, they were sitting down talking.

Well, Shelby had started talking and Laney just sort of sat and listened. Why? Because she was a good friend. The best, actually.

"If you really want to get out of this rut, you're going to have to venture out of Magnolia once in a while," Laney said. Her tone wasn't the least bit condescending and yet she certainly got her point across.

"And go where? And why? What is so great about other towns that I have to go there to have some fun?"

Laughing, Laney stood up and walked over to pat Shelby on her shoulder. "You've lived here your entire life and you have to ask that question?"

"Well...yeah."

With a sigh of her own, Laney walked around the table until she was facing Shelby. "This town is full of the people we've known all our lives. No one ever moves here! It's the same people, the same faces, the same stories! Gah!" she cried out. "Don't you want to meet someone new? Someone who doesn't know you were Miss Mini Magnolia in the second grade? Or how you had the chicken pox in middle school?"

"Maybe..."

"No maybes about it! Do you know how big the world is, Shell? Or even...just how big North Carolina is? There is so much to see and do and you never want to go anywhere! Why?"

*Good question.*

"I...I guess I'm just always busy," she said somewhat lamely. "The library keeps me busy and you know my folks always have something going on that they need help with..."

"Shell, it's time for you to start living for *you*," Laney said seriously, solemnly. "You need to have a social life. When is the last time you even went on a date?"

Ugh...she didn't even want to think about it.

"I don't know."

Laney placed both her hands on the table and leaned in a little menacingly. "It was four months ago and it was Garrett Blake." She straightened and shuddered. "He was a dork in high school and he's still a dork. Why did you go out with him again?"

Shelby shrugged.

"Shell...?" Laney prodded.

"Okay, fine. My parents set us up. They're friends with Garrett's folks and they thought we had things in common."

"The only thing the two of you have in common is you both live in Magnolia and you're both boring."

"Hey!" Shelby snapped, not even mildly amused.

"It's true! I'm not going to sugarcoat it for you! You said you're in a rut, I agreed, and now we're going to fix it!"

"How?"

"We are going out tonight and we're going to find you someone interesting to go out with!"

Shelby couldn't help snorting with disbelief. "Good luck with that. The only guys who ever seem to be attracted to me are boring, remember?"

"Not where we're going."

Laney took Shelby's hand in hers and dragged her out of the breakroom, out of the library, and out to their cars. "Where are we going?"

Grinning, Laney nudged Shelby toward her car.

"You're going to go home and find something fun to wear – not any of your librarian clothes," she clarified. "And we are going to take a ride to Wilmington to have dinner, get a couple of drinks and go dancing. Then we're..."

The loud sound of lawn equipment flared to life and blocked out whatever it was Laney was going to say. Shelby looked over her shoulder and sure enough, the landscaping crew was next door cutting their neighbor's lawn. Part of her wanted to be annoyed, but...Sam Westbrook was the one on the large mower today and...*yum*.

Tall, sandy brown hair, stubbled jaw, tanned skin, oh-so-many muscles on display through that tight, white t-shirt and a pair of snug, well-worn jeans...yeah, a woman would have to be dead not to look at Sam and think all kinds of naughty thoughts.

*I bet he tastes good too.*

She let out a quiet little hum of approval as Laney stepped in beside her.

"Ahh...good to know it's not mutual."

Shelby turned her head so quickly she felt a sharp pain in her neck. Rubbing at it irritably, she asked, "What are you talking about?"

"You just said how only boring guys are attracted to you." She shrugged. "I was beginning to wonder if that was all *you* were attracted to too." Then she nodded in Sam's direction. "I've heard Sam Westbrook described in many ways, and boring isn't one of them."

Yeah, Shelby had heard all about him too.

From just about everyone she knew.

Frowning, she forced herself to look away. "Yeah, well... it doesn't matter. I'd never go out with someone like Sam and I greatly doubt I'm his type either, so..."

Laney slapped her playfully on the shoulder. "Oh, stop. You don't know that."

Walking over to her car, she let out another sigh. "Trust me. I do. Any time I've ever been within five feet of Sam, it's like he sees right through me – like I'm not even there." She paused and hated how pathetic she sounded. "And why are we even talking about this? Don't we have plans or something?"

"We do! Just promise me something."

"Sure. What?"

"No glasses tonight. I know we already covered no librarian clothes, but that goes for the glasses too."

Reaching up, Shelby tentatively touched the frames. "You know these are just for show. They're not prescription or anything. I don't even need them."

"Then why do you wear them?"

This time her sigh was more of a huff. "We've been over this a thousand times; my parents don't know I got Lasik. They said it was a waste of money."

"Yeah, yeah, yeah...I know, but...your parents aren't here. I get why you'd wear them when you're out with them or over at their house, but...why all the time? You're going to have to tell them eventually."

"Oh, please. You know they'll give an endless lecture on how I shouldn't be so concerned about my looks and the importance of being wise with my money! And besides... basically everyone in this town has a big mouth," she said, frowning more. "You know if anyone we knew came into the library and saw me without my glasses, they'd ask why and then word would get back to my folks and...ugh. It's just easier this way. But don't worry, I won't wear them tonight."

"I'm serious, Shell, you are going to have to stand up to them eventually. You can't keep living like this."

"I know, I know. And I will. Someday. Just...not today."
She sighed and glanced one more time in Sam's direction.
He was doing nothing but riding on the large mower and
yet...he looked better than any man had a right to look.

*If only he'd look at me just once...*

"Earth to Shelby."

Quickly, Shelby averted her gaze and muttered an apology. "So, um...yeah. No glasses tonight. No worries."

"Okay. Good. So go home and grab a change of clothes
and then come to my place and we'll get ready." Then she
stopped. "On second thought, just come home with me
now."

"Why?"

"Because we both know you're going to bring something
I'm going to disagree with and you'll end up wearing something of mine anyway." She shrugged. "This just saves some
time and then we'll have more time for dinner."

"I am completely on board with that because I am
starving."

"You eat like a bird, Shell. Tonight, I'm putting my foot
down and you will eat something more than a salad for
dinner. You have to get a burger or at least a sandwich."

Inwardly, she cringed. "That's a very messy option and
how productive would it be if I have ketchup stains all
down the front of me when we hit a bar or club?"

Laney started to laugh and then nudged Shelby toward
her car. "I know you hate eating anything with your hands
so I'll give you a partial pass."

"A partial pass?"

"Uh-huh. No burgers or sandwiches, but you are eating
something other than a salad. No arguments."

"Fine," she murmured and opened her car door. "I'll
meet you back at your place."

"Sounds good."

Fifteen minutes later, they were going through Laney's closet in hopes of finding something cute for Shelby to wear. Normally she would protest, but deep down she knew Laney's wardrobe was far trendier than her own. And if she wanted to break out of this rut, some things had to change.

Like the way she dressed.

"I've got it!" Laney cried. Pulling down several hangers, she walked over to her bed and laid out her choice. "Black skinny jeans – you can never go wrong there." Then she pointed to a red, sleeveless silk shell. "We'll layer this with this super cute cropped cardigan. And I have an amazing red lace pushup bra you can wear under it! We're the same size and honestly, I bought it for myself for Christmas and never wore it so..." She was grinning from ear to ear. "What do you think?"

It wasn't horrible, but...

"I really don't look good in red. It's totally not my thing."

"And we're trying to break you of your things, so...you're wearing it."

That wasn't going to fly, so Shelby walked back over to the closet and began rummaging through until she found something a little more her style. "How about this?" She waved the hanger out the closet door. "It's still a shell and will work just the same."

"It's white, Shell," Laney replied wearily. "You need a pop of color!"

"Fine."

But it wasn't fine. It was stupid and annoying and Shelby had a feeling she was going to hate this entire night just based on one article of clothing. Stepping out of the closet, she looked at her friend with resignation.

"We'll go with the red, but if no one even talks to me or offers to buy me a drink, I'm blaming you *and* the shirt."

Laney jumped up and down excitedly, clapping her hands. "Yay! And trust me, you're going to look amazing and will have your choice of men by the end of the night!"

Shelby was still doubtful, but...something definitely had to give.

And if wearing a red top was the sacrifice she had to make, for tonight, she'd deal with it.

## 2

"I CANNOT THANK you enough for this," Sam said as he climbed into his cousin's car. "Hanging out at home with my sister on a Friday night when even my mom is out on a date was just way too depressing to deal with."

Mason Bishop let out a low laugh. "Yeah. You're certainly living the dream. Didn't you eat with them last night too?"

Sam nodded. "Yeah. And the night before. And Mom had a date both nights." He groaned. "That's why I needed to get out tonight."

They pulled out of the long driveway of their great-grandfather's home – a home Sam now shared with his mother even as it was being converted into a bed and breakfast. "How's construction coming along?"

"It's a damn mess in there," Sam replied with a shake of his head. "There's debris in just about every room because my mother can't seem to make a decision. Every time they start work somewhere, she makes them stop because she wants to change something. Then they start on another room and she does the same thing. I'm telling you, it's making me crazy."

Laughing again, Mason said, "Not nearly as crazy as it's making my mother."

"She's still pissed, huh?"

Mason nodded.

When Ezekiel Coleman – the family patriarch – passed away six months ago, he had a vast estate. There was more than enough to go around to each of his grandchildren and great-grandchildren, but the family home had gone to Sam's mother.

And Mason's mother – Sam's Aunt Georgia – was none too pleased.

Still wasn't.

"They're eventually going to have to make up, right?" Sam asked.

"You would think, but you know how stubborn my mother is. She'll be the one to carry this on way longer than it needs to."

"Everyone seemed fine over the holidays."

"It was all about appearances," Mason said. "There were too many people around for my mother to vent and gripe and complain. Plus, at that point there wasn't too much going on at the house. Now that things are seriously in motion, she's been having a fit. But she refuses to see reason on this. She got the yacht club, your mom got the house. I don't see what the big deal is. The only one her stubbornness is hurting is herself."

Sam wasn't so sure he'd call his aunt stubborn. Controlling, yes, but he couldn't say he'd ever noticed her being stubborn. Obviously, Mason knew his mother better than Sam did, so he'd have to simply agree based on that.

"Mom really misses her. I know they were never best friends, but I think part of the reason she's struggling with the decisions on the house is because this fight with your mother is weighing heavily on her. She'd probably love your mom's input on design."

"It could be a way to bridge this gap between them. Maybe if my mom feels included she'll relax a bit." He glanced over at Sam. "You should mention it to her."

He shrugged. The last thing he wanted to do was talk about his mother anymore. "Yeah, maybe." He paused. "So where are we going? Is it the place over in Wilmington we hit up last month? The one with the dance floor out on the beach?"

"Nah, too crowded for my tastes. And still too cold. A friend of mine recommended a new place. It's a little smaller, not as loud, but I thought we could check it out."

It didn't sound too promising. What he wanted tonight was the loud and crowded place where he could meet a woman who he could share a couple of drinks and dances with, and then hopefully send Mason home without him.

"You've gone quiet," his cousin commented. "I know you're in your own head and thinking this is a bad thing, but it's not. Trust me. You'll have a great time, meet someone to pass some time with, and then you'll thank me tomorrow."

"Damn. Am I *that* predictable?" Sam asked with a nervous laugh.

"A little, but I get it. When I heard about this place I wasn't too sure either, but...man, we just need something a little different tonight. I needed to get out just as much as you did, but I wasn't in the mood for the kind of place where they herd you in like cattle."

"There's an image for you," he teased.

"Yeah, right? Anyway, if we go and we're not into it, there are plenty of other bars we can check out. No point in driving an hour and not making the most of it."

The rest of the ride was spent making small talk about work. Mason worked for the city in their planning and engineering department. For years, all everyone talked about was how Mason was going to follow in his father's footsteps and be a lawyer, and then someday, mayor. But his cousin had surprised everyone when he announced he wasn't going to law school so he could forge his own path.

It was about that time that Sam actually felt a kinship to him that they'd never had before.

Growing up, Sam could admit he and his cousin were never close. If anything, Sam kind of hated him, but it was mainly because whenever they were visiting in Magnolia and spending time with the whole family, all everyone talked about was how great Mason was.

He and Mallory had nicknamed him Mason the Magnificent.

Hey, they were ten when they came up with it, so...

In the last year or so, Sam saw another side to his cousin and...well...turns out he was kind of cool. And if his parents ever took their clutches off him for a bit, he was sure Mason could be freaking awesome. And happy!

"How are things going with the rebuilding? You're on the committee for all that, right?" Damn. Maybe he should pay more attention to the things going on.

Mason nodded. "Yeah. So far, everything's going great. We received disaster relief funds and the community has really pulled together to get Magnolia Sound back on track and possibly even better than it ever was." He paused and groaned before reaching over and punching Sam.

"Ow! What was that for?"

"Don't make me talk about work when we're going out to have fun and hopefully get laid," he grumbled. "My job is currently sucking my will to live and as I was answering your question, I instantly slipped into politician mode – like I was speaking at a press conference or something."

That had Sam laughing. "Well, I didn't want to be the one to say it, but...yeah. That's exactly what you sounded like."

Luckily Mason didn't take offense. "Someday maybe I'll be able to speak like a real boy and not this puppet my father made me."

They both went quiet for several minutes. When the sign for the city limits of Wilmington came into view, Sam felt relieved. "Okay, so this place is smaller and a little quieter, but is it like a pub? A bistro? A club?"

"Yes to all the above," Mason said with a grin. "The way my buddy Paul explained it, it's a little bit of all of that. They have food – small plate kind of stuff – and a great bar, a nice semi-outdoor area with a firepit and that sort of thing, and when I asked about dancing, he said they have that too. It's just smaller and a little more upscale so you don't get the college crowd hanging around as much."

Okay, now he was a little more interested.

And thirty minutes later, he was really glad he'd kept a somewhat open mind because the place was amazing. Just as Mason had described, it was smaller, more intimate, and he could hear himself think and carry on a conversation.

"Good call, man," he said to his cousin, raising his beer to him. "And there is a good crowd here tonight for sure."

"Agreed," Mason said, scanning the crowd. He nodded toward the dancefloor. "You know I'm not much for dancing, but the blonde over there in the hot pink just waved me over. I'll see you later." And with another nod, he was gone.

Sam looked around and had to admit, there were definitely some beautiful women here tonight, but who did he want to strike up a conversation with? He turned to put his beer back on the table when someone collided right into him. *"Oof!"* He reached out to steady them and found himself face-to-face with the answer to all his prayers.

*Beautiful*, that was his first impression.

Long dark hair that was highlighted with three of his favorite things: honey, caramel, and whiskey. Big hazel eyes he could already see flecks of green and blue in. And deep red lips that...well, his mind was already envisioning where he'd like to see them.

*Damn.*

His hands were on her bare arms and her skin felt like warm silk. "You okay?" he forced himself to ask.

Turning her head to her left and to her right before returning her gaze to his, she asked, "Who, me?"

He laughed softly. "Yeah. You." He smiled. "I didn't see you there when I turned around. I hope I didn't hurt you."

She looked adorably flustered but didn't move away. "Um...yes. Thank you. I'm fine." With a slight shake of her head, she explained, "I knew these shoes would do me in. I'm afraid I tripped and banged into you, so maybe I should be asking if you're okay or if I hurt you." A small smile played across those sexy lips and Sam was instantly infatuated.

Taking one hand from her arm, he placed it over his heart. "Well, if we're being honest, I did get a little hurt."

The soft gasp hit him first.

Then her look of utter devastation.

"Oh, my gosh! I am so sorry," she said, her voice going a little breathless and definitely laced with concern. "I...I...are you okay? Can I get you something? Do you need to sit down?"

His conscience got the better of him and he knew he needed to put her mind at ease. "It's okay, really, I...I was just kidding. I'm fine, I swear."

She visibly relaxed and this time she did move out of his grasp. "Oh. Okay. Um...good." With a slight pause, she added, "Have a good night." But when she went to walk away, Sam stopped her. She turned and her eyes looked a little sad and he had to wonder why.

"I'm sorry," he said. "I thought I was being funny. I didn't mean to upset you. Can I buy you a drink?"

She blinked several times as if she didn't understand the question and Sam began to wonder if he should have just let her walk away. "You want to buy me a drink?"

Did he stutter?

Nodding, he said, "Yeah. I'd like to. What can I get you?" And without waiting for a response, he took her by the hand and walked her over to the bar. He ordered another beer for himself while she ordered a Malibu cocktail. Very girly, he thought, but it totally fit. While they waited for their drinks they talked about the atmosphere, the crowd level, and once he paid the tab, Sam didn't think twice about taking her by her hand again and leading her outside to the firepit area.

There were two other couples out there, but they found a bench of their own flanked by heat lamps and sat down. She took a sip of her drink and sighed happily. "This is so much better out here, don't you think?"

He couldn't agree more. Between the outside lighting

and the light of the fire, he could really see her face – which looked even more beautiful than it had inside. Nodding, he asked, "Come here often?"

As soon as the words were out of his mouth, he regretted them because they were beyond clichéd. She must have thought so too because they both started to laugh.

Sam bowed his head and shook it, even as he continued to laugh. "Wow, I'm…I'm so sorry. That was completely cheesy."

His beautiful stranger placed one hand on his leg. "Just a little." But she was still giggling softly too.

Lifting his head, their eyes met and he swore the rest of the world seemed to fade away. Not once in his life could he ever remember feeling like this. He'd been instantly attracted to women in the past, but that was just lust. What he was feeling right now was much stronger than that and if he could, he'd whisk her away to someplace private so he could talk to her and find out everything about her.

*Yikes…should probably drink this beer a lot slower because clearly I'm already drunk.*

Would it be wrong to reach up, cup her face, and kiss her?

She licked her lips as if reading his mind and Sam had to stifle a groan. Did she have any idea how sexy she was?

Clearing his throat, he tried to think of something to say that wouldn't sound too ridiculous. "So, uh…I'm Sam, by the way." He smiled and couldn't wait for her to formally introduce herself. Her smile fell slightly and she stared at him oddly for the just briefest of moments and yet…he was mildly curious as to what put that look on her face.

Her smile was back as she squared her shoulders. "I'm Shelby."

"That's a beautiful name," he said, leaning toward her.

"And totally fitting." The slight flush to her cheeks totally captivated him and as he shifted a little closer to her, he could smell her perfume. Unable to help himself, he inhaled deeply and knew he was coming on strong, but...he couldn't stop.

Carefully, Shelby moved to put a little distance between them and Sam was afraid he had totally crossed a line. The only thing he could do was try to get them back to where they were a minute ago and reel in his strong reaction to her. "Okay, without being too much of a cliché, do you live around here?"

And silently prayed the answer was yes.

"No," she said, that odd look back on her face. "How about you?"

Resting his arm along the back of their bench, he replied, "Me either. I'm from a small town north of here. Magnolia Sound. Ever been there?"

She gave him a small smile. "I've heard of it."

"Yeah? That's cool. So, uh...why don't you tell me a little about yourself," he said and wanted to kick himself. He was usually much smoother than this.

And Shelby seemed to sense that too because she gave him a sassy little smirk. "I didn't realize we were already at the interview portion of the evening," she said, her smile growing. She took a sip of her drink and relaxed against the back of their bench. "But you should go first."

"Me?" he croaked, and when she nodded, he figured he might as well get it over with. Clearing his throat again, Sam eyed his beer and took one pull just to wet his throat a bit. "Well, uh...like I said, I live in Magnolia Sound. Just moved there about three months ago." And from there he went on to tell her about his business and a little about his family. By the time he was done, he felt like he had been talking all night. Thankfully, it was Shelby's turn now.

"Now, how about a little about you," he said casually, and almost choked when she stood up. Was that it? Had he bored her to death? Turned her off already? It couldn't be! Dropping his beer, Sam all but jumped to his feet and watched in horror as Shelby flinched away from him. "Uh... hey. Where are...um...where are you going? Can I get you another drink?"

*Creepy, dude. You have officially become creepy.*

Shelby made a bit of a face at him and reached for his hand. "I was going to ask if you wanted to dance."

---

*I'm dancing with Sam Westbrook.*

*Sam Westbrook's arms are around me.*

*Oh, my god...did Sam Westbrook just smell my hair?!*

So many thoughts raced through Shelby's mind and she had to fight to keep calm. When she bumped into Sam earlier, it had been a complete coincidence. And when he made the comment on how he hadn't seen her there, she had to fight the urge to run off and cry. But once he started talking to her, however, she warred between being super excited and incredibly disappointed.

He had no idea who she was.

Not the biggest confidence boost, but...there it was.

Although, it really didn't matter right now because there was a slow and sultry song playing, she was in Sam's arms and he smelled amazing. Even if he suddenly realized who she was and how he saw her at least once a week in town and decided he wasn't interested, she would be okay.

The last thirty minutes with him completely made her night.

So would spending another thirty minutes with him, but hey, she wasn't going to be picky.

When one song turned into two and Sam made no move to leave the dance floor, Shelby felt like the luckiest girl in the world. Of course this current mood couldn't last. This was a club and to have two slow songs in a row was a bit of an oddity. Still, who was she to argue if the DJ wanted to keep this up all night. She'd dance for hours if it meant she was doing it with Sam.

As if privy to her inner thoughts, he pulled her closer and murmured in her ear, "Eventually you're going to have to tell me something about you." His breath felt warm and wonderful and made her tremble a little. "I want to know all about you, Shelby."

It was on the tip of her tongue to make a snarky comment about how she doubted he'd want to hear about the life of a librarian, but opted to keep that comment to herself. However, she did feel the need to say, "There really isn't much to tell. Trust me when I say it sounds like your life is way more exciting."

He laughed softly and that gently vibration felt oddly satisfying against her.

"Oh, I'll bet you're more exciting than you think," he said softly, his lips perilously close to her ear. "If I had to wager, I'd say you are possibly the most exciting woman I've ever met."

Oh, he's good, she thought, and her foolish heart seriously skipped a beat at his cheesy line. She had to admit, she wasn't sure what to expect if she ever found herself in this kind of situation with Sam, and now that she was here, it was more amusing than a turn on.

That was bad, wasn't it?

The song ended and, as predicted, a more upbeat one came on. As if of one mind, she and Sam walked back to the firepit area and found they had it all to themselves. He offered to get her another drink and Shelby readily accepted and volunteered to hold their spot. Once he was out of sight, she almost screamed when Laney bounced in the spot beside her.

"Oh, my God! Was that Sam Westbrook you were just dancing with?" she asked excitedly.

Nodding, she said, "Yes. Yes, it was." And then broke out into a fit of giggles.

Laney laughed along with her for a second before sobering. "Wait, what's so funny about that?"

"Oh, Laney, where do I even begin?" she said, trying to catch her breath. "It's so weird that he's even here after we were talking about him earlier!"

"True, but..."

"And he's funny and charming and has the worst pick-up lines ever!"

"No!"

Nodding again, she said, "Oh, yes. I'm telling you, it's almost like *he's* nervous! He babbles just like I do when... well, like I do! It's crazy!"

"Aww...I think that's kind of cute! Maybe you *do* make him nervous. Have you even thought about that?"

"Oh, please. Can you imagine? A guy like Sam – a guy who has dated a large amount of the Magnolia Sound female population – is nervous around the shyest girl in town. Right."

"Don't be too sure," Laney argued lightly. "The way he was looking at you while you were dancing was pretty damn hot!" She fanned herself dramatically.

Shelby looked toward the bar to see if he was on his way back before looking at her friend again. "So what about you? How's your night going?"

"Met a super cute guy who is currently getting me a Cosmo. We're going to order a little something to eat and get to know each other some more. He's an IT guy here in Wilmington, his name is Tom and...so far he seems really nice."

"Well good for us!" Shelby said, smiling. "I guess it was a good night to break out of our ruts, huh?"

Laney patted her knee lightly. "*Our* ruts? Sweetie, that was all you. I am in no way, shape, or form in a rut." She paused and looked around, her eyes going wide. "Here comes your sexy landscaper." Jumping to her feet, she gave Shelby a thumbs up. "Have fun!"

A minute later, Sam handed her her drink. "Here you go. Hope I wasn't gone too long."

Accepting it, she thanked him. "Not at all. Although I think it's gotten more crowded in there. I'm kind of glad we're outside."

He nodded. "I'm sure it won't be long before the crowd spills out this way and we lose having the fire all to ourselves."

She did hate the thought of that.

"Well, if that happens, we'll maybe have to think about moving to another spot or maybe dancing again."

Sam moved in closer and reached out to touch her hair. Tonight she had straightened it because Laney said it looked good that way. Normally she wore it clipped up in a ponytail or let it be naturally wavy, but that wasn't the look she was going for tonight. All around, this evening felt a little like an out-of-body experience. She was dressed in clothes she normally didn't wear, her makeup was heavier than the way she normally applied it, and she had the hottest man in town giving her all his attention.

Maybe she fell asleep early and this was all a dream. "Shelby?"

Her name on Sam's lips pulled her out of her inner thoughts. "Hmm?"

"What's your favorite thing to do on the weekends?"

The question took her a little by surprise. Thinking about it for all of five seconds, she said, "I love having a lazy day out on the boat."

And her answer seemed to surprise him because his dark brown eyes went wide. "Really? You sail?"

She nodded. "Uh-huh. Practically since I was twelve. My folks bought a boat and made sure I knew everything about it. I have a small one of my own and I don't go out on it nearly as much as I'd like to."

"How come?"

She shrugged. "There always seems to be something else to do – work around the house, grocery shopping…and really, it's not smart to go out sailing alone."

"Very true. We have a boat as well and I don't go out nearly as much as I'd like, either."

The image of the two of them sitting out alone on the deck of her boat with no distractions and no one else around popped into Shelby's mind and it was all she could do to keep from asking him to do that with her tomorrow.

"What about you?" she asked instead. "What's your favorite thing to do on the weekends?"

The sexy grin he gave her said it all and Shelby felt herself blush. There were promises in his smile and for a minute, she wanted to pretend she was the first girl he was making those promises to. Unfortunately, she knew it wasn't true. So many girls she knew had a Sam Westbrook story.

Granted, many of them were from years ago but there were enough current ones going around that she had to work to remind herself that this was just who he was – a consummate flirt with a short attention span.

And for tonight, his attention was on her so...why not enjoy it?

"When I'm not working, I do enjoy going out sailing but, like I said, I don't do it as much as I'd like." He let out a long breath and his expression went a little serious. "I used to love just hanging around and being lazy – waking up on a Saturday with no plan or direction and seeing where the day took me. With all the work we're doing on the house converting it into a bed and breakfast, it seems like there's never a day without having to lend a hand with it. I long for the days when I don't wake up to power tools buzzing somewhere in the house."

"I'm sure that's incredibly disruptive," she said softly, reaching out and placing her hand on his and loving how warm his skin was. "How much longer is it going to take?"

"Wish I knew," he murmured with a slight shake of his head. "My mother is being a little indecisive and that's why every room in the house is a construction zone rather than just a few at a time. Even now, my room is a complete mess."

"So...you live with just your mom?"

Shelby could have sworn he started to blush before he responded. "Like I said, I moved back three months ago thanks to my great-grandfather's will. At the time, I knew what my mother was planning on doing with the house, but I didn't think she'd be doing it so soon." He paused. "I have a twin sister..."

"Twins? Really?" How had she not known this? She

knew he had a sister – had even met Mallory a time or two – but never realized they were twins.

Smiling, he said, "Yup. Fraternal." He paused. "Mallory's here now too but she recently moved in with her fiancé so now it's just me and mom in the big ol' construction zone of a house." He laughed softly. "I swear, Pops would be having a fit if he saw the mess the place is in right now."

She squeezed his hand. "Maybe, but I'm sure he's happy knowing your mom is going to turn it into something amazing."

"Sure. If it ever gets finished." He winked at her and moved in closer. They were pressed together from shoulder to hip to thigh and it felt so good that Shelby had to suppress a little moan of pleasure. "Shelby?" his voice was now low and gruff and she knew whatever it was he was going to ask, it wasn't going to be about a few of her favorite things.

Looking up at him, she let out a soft gasp at his intense expression. His eyes were so dark they were almost black. She swallowed hard and licked her lips. "Hmm?"

"I'd really like to kiss you," he whispered, even as his lips were practically against hers.

"That's good," she responded, not recognizing the breathy sound of her own voice. "Because I'd really like for you to kiss me."

Sam hesitated and she was afraid he was having second thoughts – like maybe he finally recognized her – but then everything changed. The world around them stopped. The music faded away and his tongue gently licked along her bottom lip even as one of his arms wrapped around her shoulder and pressed her even closer to him. It was like it was happening in slow motion until it wasn't.

Once his lips pressed against hers, it was like nothing

she had ever experienced before. Shelby was used to slow kisses that built up to something deeper...wetter. But that wasn't how Sam kissed at all. He started deep and wet and kept going from there. She felt swept away and yet unsure of what she was supposed to do. This wasn't what she was used to and rather than being able to relax and go with the flow, she felt herself go tense.

Maybe it was the fact that they were in such a public setting and everything in his kiss was not meant to be seen that way. His kiss felt dark and erotic and...definitely something to be saved for behind closed doors. Before she knew it, she was pushing away and...

"I'm sorry," she whispered, scooting out of his embrace. "I...I'm sorry. I can't do this."

The stunned expression on his face told her he was confused – probably because no woman in her right mind would turn away from a man who could kiss like that.

But she wasn't like that.

And right now, she hated that about herself.

"I...I should go." She stood up and spotted Laney across the room and gave her a frantic look to convey her desperate need to escape. She was on the move when Sam seemed to snap out of his own stupor and came after her.

"Shelby? Wait!" He reached out and gently grasped her arm and she stopped and faced him. "I...I'm sorry. I didn't mean to come on so strong. Please don't leave."

It was so tempting to stay – to go back and sit with him and just pretend like she didn't freak out mere seconds ago.

But it was too late.

He'd already seen how he was clearly out of her league and why stay and risk embarrassing herself even further?

Shaking her head, she pulled away. "I really need to go."

Forcing herself to meet his gaze, she felt herself begin to weaken.

*No! A man like Sam Westbrook is more than you can handle. Why are you trying to fool yourself?*

"It was nice meeting you, Sam."

And then she ran through the bar and straight for the exit and silently hoped Laney was right behind her.

3

Two weeks later Sam had to wonder if he'd imagined the whole encounter. He'd gone back to Wilmington multiple times and yet he hadn't seen Shelby since.

It was maddening.

How could he not have gotten her last name? It was a rookie mistake! He'd asked everyone who worked at the club if they knew who she was with no success. He literally had nothing to go on. They didn't talk about anything specific to her and every time he thought about it, he got angrier with himself. There was nothing he could do and – as much as it pained him – he had no choice but to try to move on.

And yet...he couldn't.

Mason had texted him earlier about going out tonight – to somewhere completely different so he'd stop being a borderline-creepy stalker – and Sam turned him down.

Why? Why this girl? He should be able to forget about her! It was one kiss! One kiss that had clearly freaked her out, but...for some reason her reaction to it brought out the protective side of himself that he didn't even know existed.

If he could, he'd apologize profusely, beg for her forgiveness, and be willing to take things as slow as she wanted him to.

Again, which was completely out of character for him. In the past, if a girl wasn't interested, Sam was more than happy to move on. He didn't chase after women. That totally wasn't his thing and, to be honest, he never had to chase anyone.

But he'd totally be willing to chase after Shelby.

If only he knew where to start.

It was a Thursday afternoon and he was hitting all the commercial properties along Main Street just like he did every week. The weather was finally starting to warm up a bit and, because most of these accounts had been on bi-weekly or even monthly maintenance in the winter, he now needed to take the time to speak with each account and modify their calendars for the spring and summer months. This was the kind of work he loathed, but it was better than sitting on a mower with nothing to do but think about ways to try to find Shelby.

So he'd walk and talk and plug dates in on his tablet. He'd smile and make small talk and hopefully at the end of the day he wouldn't be ready to die of boredom or frustration.

It was like he had said to Mallory only a few weeks ago – the people of Magnolia were judgmental where he was concerned. Things were getting mildly better, but it seemed as soon as he let himself relax he found himself listening to someone else's recounting of something he did when he was a kid. It was beyond frustrating. Out riding the equipment, he could ignore them or simply pretend he didn't see their disapproving looks and he didn't have to hear their disapproving tones. And yeah, he might pretend like it was no big deal, but...it was. No one likes knowing people hate them, right? Or knowing how everyone thinks you're a loser. Now he was going to have look some of those very people in the eye and see exactly how they felt all the while doing his best to be a professional businessman.

And hopefully not punch anyone in the face.

His first stop was at Mallory's shop. It was totally the coward's way out but he needed a little something to bolster his confidence.

"Hey!" his sister called out to him when he walked in. She had the beach décor shop – the only one in town – which had been left to her by their great-grandfather. Unlike Sam, Mallory willingly accepted her inheritance and gave up her job and career up in New York to move to Magnolia. Of course, her decision was made a little easier by the fact that Jake Summerford – now Mallory's fiancé – was here. "What's up?"

Shrugging, he made his way across the showroom. Any item you'd possibly need to decorate a coastal house was here – all kinds of knick-knacks, paintings, and small pieces of furniture. His sister was loving it and it showed on her face. "I'm making the rounds getting everyone ready for the spring and summer schedule since we'll be going back to weekly visits now that the warmer weather is approaching."

Nodding, Mallory walked over and hugged him. "Got time for a cup of coffee?"

As if on cue, he felt a bit of a chill wrack his body. "Sure. Why not?" As they walked across the large room, Sam continued to take it all in. "Have you thought about changing the name of this place? You know, now that Barb has officially retired and you've been running it for a while?"

Mallory shrugged. "I have, but I haven't come up with the perfect name yet. I want it to be something creative and fun and..." She sighed and gave him a lopsided grin. "I've been a little distracted."

He didn't even want to think about what she was referring to.

In the back corner, there was a small coffee station set up. "Got any big plans this weekend?" She glanced at him over her shoulder as she placed one pod in her Keurig. "You and Mason have been hitting the clubs hard the last couple of weeks."

For a minute, Sam didn't confirm or deny her comment, but then thought maybe his sister was the perfect person to talk to about this Shelby situation. He walked over to a small dinette set and sat down. "Can I ask you something?"

"Sure," she replied happily as she fussed around getting their drinks ready.

"I met a girl a couple of weeks ago," he began and then told her about the night he met Shelby and how it all ended.

Collapsing in the chair beside him, she looked at him with wide eyes. "Seriously? She just...ran?"

"Unfortunately, yes."

"Wow."

"I know."

"So...what are you going to do?"

Did she not understand the entire story he just told her? "Um...Mal? That's what I need your help with!" He let out a long breath. "I've gone back to the club multiple times and haven't seen her since! What do I do? How do I find her?"

Mallory let out a laugh or maybe it was a snort, but either way, she was looking at him like he was crazy. "How should I know?" She shook her head. "I have no idea. I mean, you have nothing to go on! You don't have her last name and you don't know where she lives...did you do anything but talk about yourself all night?"

It was one thing when the people around town looked down on him, but it really bothered him when his sister had such a low opinion of him.

"Thanks, Mal," he said with disgust, standing up. He moved all of three steps before she jumped in front of him.

"Okay, stop! Geez...why are you so damn sensitive lately?" she demanded, equally annoyed with him as he was with her. "You're never like this! And you can't blame me for questioning you, Sam. Based on everything you said, that's what it seemed like!"

Raking a hand through his hair, he growled with frustration even if he had to agree with her. "Okay, fine. I can see why you'd think that, but...I don't know, she never seemed to answer any questions about herself!"

Mallory studied him for a moment before nudging him back toward the table and their coffee. Once they were seated, she said, "Doesn't that seem a little odd to you?"

"What do you mean?"

"I just think it's odd that someone would avoid answering any questions about themselves unless there's a good reason."

Frowning, he took a sip of his coffee. "Like what kind of reason could there possibly be? Or for that matter, why not just lie? How would I even know the difference?"

Shrugging, she suggested, "Maybe she wasn't really looking for anything beyond a couple of drinks? Maybe she has a boyfriend? Or...and I know you're going to take offense to this but...maybe she really wasn't that into you."

Sam clenched his jaw so tightly he was amazed he didn't break it. Yeah, all those things had gone through his mind at one point or another, but he pushed them all away.

For starters, Shelby didn't seem like the kind of girl who would be out trolling for a one-night stand or anything like that. She was too shy, too sweet, and if he based it simply on their kiss, she was a little too inexperienced for that sort of behavior.

The boyfriend theory? Nuh-uh. Next!

And not into him? No way. There was so much chemistry between them that it wasn't even possible that she was faking it or that he misread it. She had said she wanted him to kiss her and besides...everything else told him she was just as attracted to him as he was to her.

The touch of Mallory's hand on his snapped him out of his reverie. "You're really into this girl, aren't you?"

It wasn't a question.

With a mirthless laugh, he lifted his mug. "Crazy, right? I spent maybe two hours with her. Am I obsessing about this because she took off or is it something more?" He paused. "It's not possible for me to be feeling what I think I'm feeling."

"What do you think you're feeling?" she asked carefully.

He stared at his sister for a long moment. "There was a connection there, Mal. I've never had something like that happen to me before. I took one look at her and felt like...*Bam!*" He slapped a hand on his chest. "If I could have conjured up the girl of my dreams, it was Shelby."

"Shelby?"

He nodded. "Yeah, Shelby. Didn't I say her name before?"

Mallory shook her head. "No, but..."

"But what?"

She shrugged and then waved him off. "It's nothing. It's a very pretty name."

Sam smiled. "She's a very pretty girl."

Letting out a long sigh, Mallory slouched down in seat. "Well...damn."

"Tell me about it."

They sat like that in companionable silence until they both finished their coffees. "So what are you going to do?" Mallory finally asked.

He stared down into his mug. "There really isn't anything I can do. And it pisses me off more than you know."

The sound of the bell over the front door ringing had them both turning around. Two older women walked in and Mallory instantly rose to her feet and smoothed the front of her dress. Sam knew she needed to get back to work so he needed to move on to his next customer and get on with the fall schedule.

Sam took their mugs to the back room and washed them so his sister wouldn't have to – or maybe he was just procrastinating.

Maybe.

By the time he walked back through the shop, he resigned himself to his plans for the afternoon and waved to Mallory on his way out the door. Out on the sidewalk, he looked to his left and then to his right and figured it didn't matter which way he went; he had more than enough people to talk to and even if he only spent a few minutes with most of them, he still had a couple of hours ahead of him.

With a sigh of resignation, Sam checked his phone and saw there weren't any messages. Pulling his sunglasses from his pocket, he turned to the right, made his way to the corner and then crossed the street. His first stop would be Henderson's Bakery. Mrs. Henderson was one of the few exceptions in his book – she was nice and normally insisted on giving him an apple turnover or a glazed donut whenever he stopped by on business.

There were worse places to start.

---

"Did you lose a bet or something?"

Shelby looked up from the computer and blinked at Laney. "Excuse me?"

"In the last two weeks, you are dressing more and more like my Great-aunt Ruth." She paused and wrinkled her nose. "And she's ninety-three. So what gives?"

"I don't know what you're talking about."

Laney snorted with disbelief and stepped around the desk. "You know exactly what I'm talking about. Ever since you kissed Sam…"

"Would you be quiet?!" she hissed quietly, stepping in close. "Now isn't the time to talk about that."

Laney rolled her eyes. "Shell, what do you think is going to happen if we talk about it? Hell, you haven't talked about it at all since you ran out of the bar that night! I was on the other side of the room and saw the two of you kiss and then you freaked out, but you won't tell me why!" Then she grabbed Shelby's arm, dragged her to the breakroom and shut the door.

"We both can't be back here! Someone needs to be at the desk!"

Opening the door, Laney yelled out, "Jules? Can you man the desk for five minutes? Thanks!" before slamming the door shut again. "There. Satisfied?"

Pouting, Shelby sat down and crossed her arms, refusing to answer.

Slowly walking across the room, Laney frowned at her. "Did he hurt you?"

Her eyes went wide. "What? No, of course not!"

"Did he insult you?"

She shook her head.

"Then what, Shelby?" she demanded. "Something had to have happened for you to run out of there and away from Sam like that! We've known each other since the third grade and I've never seen you do something like that." Cautiously, she sat down beside her and took one of Shelby's hands in hers. "Whatever it is, you can tell me."

And just like that tears stung her eyes and it just made her want to cry even more. How ridiculous was that? Wanting to cry made her want to cry even though she didn't want to cry! *Gah!* This was what her life had been like for the last two weeks! She had refused to tell Laney why she was upset and then refused to talk about it ever since. But maybe she needed to get it off her chest so she could move on.

Softly clearing her throat, she said, "All night Sam had been asking about me – about my life – and I kept sidestepping the answer."

"Why?"

She sighed. "Because he didn't know who I was! He had no idea that I'm the girl at the library he sees every damn week but doesn't acknowledge! At first I thought it was funny, but as the night went on it kind of bothered me."

"O-kay..."

"But...part of me thought it was a blessing because... well...it's obvious he's not usually interested in a girl like me and because I looked different that night, he was. So if I could hold his interest for a little while, I thought it would be enough."

Laney looked at her sympathetically. "I get all that, Shell, I do. But it still doesn't explain why you bolted the way you did."

She threw her head back and stared up at the ceiling for a moment. "Then he kissed me."

When Laney was quiet, Shelby straightened and looked at her and waited for her response.

"Was he a bad kisser? Because I have to tell you, he doesn't look like he'd be a bad kisser," Laney said after a minute.

Shaking her head, she frowned. "No, he's a good kisser. A great kisser. An amazing kisser."

"Did he have bad breath?"

"What? No!"

"Did you?"

"That's ridiculous..."

"Then what's the problem, Shelby! You were into him, he was into you, no one had bad breath, and he's an amazing kisser! I don't see a problem here!"

"That was the problem."

"Huh? You've lost me."

"He kissed like...like..." She groaned and rested her head on the table while Laney placed a reassuring hand on her shoulder. "I've never been kissed like that!"

"Oh, sweetie..."

"It was so intimate and sexy and possessive," she explained. "It felt like it was too much to be doing in public and I panicked. Then I froze." She paused. "And then I ran." Forcing herself to sit up, a few stray tears rolled down her cheek. "I'm so embarrassed."

"Wow. I don't know what to say," Laney said quietly.

"That's why I've been dressing more conservatively

than usual. I'm afraid I'll see him somewhere and he'll recognize me."

"You didn't look *that* different, Shell. I mean, your hair was down and you didn't have on your glasses, but you're still you. If he got close enough, he'd know who you are."

She didn't believe that. Once a week, every week, for the last three months she had seen Sam working in the yard next door and she knew she had a tendency to stop and stare, but he never noticed her. She'd run into him in the grocery store too. Well...she didn't really *run* into him, but they'd been there at the same time and...he didn't notice her. Then there was the time they were both waiting for their pizza at Michael's Italian Restaurant and he stood three feet away from her for a solid ten minutes and never even acknowledged her.

But after sitting with him so closely that night, she knew there was a good chance if he saw her now he'd recognize her. So she wore less makeup than usual, pulled her hair back more severely, and dressed so her figure was hidden as much as possible. She hated every second of it, but...she was in self-preservation mode. In another week or two she figured she could relax a bit because she had no doubt Sam would move on to someone else by that time.

And just the thought of that made her feel sick to her stomach.

She sniffled and wiped away the tears. "I'm pathetic, right?"

Laney grabbed her and hugged her. "No, you're not pathetic," she said fiercely before pulling back. "You are an incredibly good and sweet and kind person. There is not one thing wrong with you and don't you ever forget it!"

That made Shelby smile. "Well, you have to say that.

You're my best friend and best friends have to say things like that."

Laughing, Laney hugged her one more time before she stood up. "Is there anything I can do?"

Shelby let out a long breath. "I wish. Eventually I'll get over my embarrassment and not feel like I have to look over my shoulder every time I go out in town."

"I wish you didn't feel that way."

"Me too."

They walked back out onto the floor and Shelby went to her spot behind the desk and Laney took the book cart and went about placing books back on the shelves.

When their shift was over two hours later, they walked out the front door together. "What are you going to do tonight?" Laney asked. "Want to grab some dinner?"

"Thanks, but I'm just feeling a little drained. I think I'm going to grab some Chinese food on the way home, put on my jammies and a movie, and just chill. Sorry."

Laney waved her off. "No worries. That actually sounds like a good idea. Maybe I'll..."

"Shelby! Phone call for you! It's Mrs. Martin from the senior center! She wants to talk to you about volunteers!"

Turning around, they saw Julie standing in the entryway with the phone in her hand and Shelby groaned. "Couldn't she just tell them I was gone for the day?" she murmured. Unfortunately, she knew she needed to take the call, and after wishing Laney a good night, she jogged back toward Julie.

Twenty minutes later, her head was pounding and she all but threw the phone at Julie on her way out the door. While it was important to work together within the community, at times it could be extremely trying. Mrs. Martin wanted Shelby to encourage the seniors to come in and volunteer at the library. And while it sounded very sweet, it was a scheduling and logistical nightmare.

Then she felt guilty for thinking like that.

"Chinese food and jammies," she murmured as she walked toward her car. Off in the distance she heard a lawn-mower start up and nearly jumped out of her skin. Picking up her pace, she tripped and fumbled for her keys and cursed when both she and the keys fell to the ground. And just as she grabbed them, her glasses slid off. A string of curses came out of her mouth before she could stop them. Her knees were now skinned and burning and she silently prayed no one noticed her fall. With a steadying breath, Shelby told herself to calm down. Slowly she came to her feet and took all of one step before she nearly fell over again due to the pain in her knee. Stumbling a few feet, she screamed when someone steadied her from behind.

"Hey, are you okay?" a male voice said from behind her.

And not just any male voice, *the* male voice.

Oh. No.

Shelby stiffened and dreaded turning around but there was no way to avoid it. Pushing her glasses firmly up on her nose, she nodded. "Um...yes. Thanks," she said quietly, keeping her head down and hoping her voice didn't give her away.

Sam took a step back to give her some space and asked, "Are you sure? It looked like you fell pretty hard."

*You have no idea*, she wanted to say.

Nodding, she reached into her purse, grabbed her sunglasses and quickly slipped them on.

Right over her regular glasses.

"Um...," he began. "Are you sure you're supposed to wear them like that?"

"What?" Reaching up, Shelby realized what she'd done

and tried to switch them out. But as soon as both her glasses were off, she realized her mistake.

"Shelby?" he asked, and there was no hiding the shock in his tone. "What...? I mean, how...?"

Her shoulders sagged and she let out a weary sigh as she met his gaze. "Hi, Sam."

His dark eyes were wide and his mouth was pretty much hanging open and it was obvious he didn't know what to say.

*Probably horrified to see you in your natural state.*

Yeah. Probably.

He shook his head slightly and seemed to snap out of his stupor. "What are you doing here?" He looked over her shoulder toward the library and then back to her. "Wait..." And she knew the instant it all came together for him. "You work here."

She nodded.

"I've seen you out here before," he said, more to himself than to her.

She nodded again.

"But...why didn't you mention that when we met? You never said you worked here in Magnolia. If anything, you made it sound like you had only heard of the place!" His voice grew a little louder with each word.

Of all the ways Shelby envisioned running into Sam would go, him being angry wasn't one of them.

"I...it just seemed..."

"You let me go on and on that night about where I lived and you never let on that I was pretty much wasting my time!"

"I wouldn't say you were wasting..."

He took a step back and growled with frustration.

"Why would you lie about it? What was the harm in saying you worked here?"

"It wasn't just that..."

"Do you live here too?" he asked angrily. "Did you know who I was when you banged into me?"

"Okay, I didn't exactly *bang* into you..."

Throwing up his hands in disgust, he said, "You know what? It doesn't even matter. Whatever." He started to walk away but turned around one more time. "And you know what's worse is how you're not even *trying* to defend yourself or tell me I'm wrong. So...yeah. Whatever. See ya."

This time when he walked away, Shelby sprang into action and grabbed his arm. "Hey!" she yelled. When he turned and looked at her, his angry glare was no deterrent. "If you would have shut up for five seconds, maybe I could have finished a sentence!"

Sam pulled free of her grasp and crossed his arms over his chest.

And it was totally inappropriate of her to fixate on just how muscular they were.

"Yes, I knew who you were that night, but not until after you turned around and started talking to me," she hurriedly explained. "As to why I didn't mention living here, well...I found it a little insulting that you didn't know who I was!"

"*What?!*" he cried. "How would I know? We've never met!"

"You seem to know every other female in this town!" she snapped and her hands immediately flew to her mouth. How could she be so stupid as to blurt something like that out? Was she crazy?

His eyes narrowed at her. "Excuse me?"

Shelby braced herself for more angry words but instead

he seemed to look...defeated. He took one step back and then another.

"Yeah," he said quietly. "That's me." Another few steps. "Why should you be any different?" And for some reason, that last part seemed more to himself than to her. Turning, he walked back toward where his crew was working.

She stood there mutely for a solid minute before she slowly took off after him. When she caught up, Sam was standing on the lawn and calling out directions to his crew. For the life of her she had no idea how they heard him over the noise of all the equipment, but they seemed to. When he turned to walk away, he walked right into her. His strong hands reached out and grasped her arms instinctively, but as soon as he saw she was okay, he simply moved around her and kept walking.

This time she put a little pep in her step to catch up. He was opening the door to his truck when she called out his name. She was a little breathless and her knee was killing her, but luckily, he stopped and waited for her.

"Okay, look," she began, hating how out of breath she sounded. "You're right. I should have been up front and honest with you, but...look at me." For emphasis, she motioned to her entire body. "You've seen me around town before and never noticed me. I'm a plain-looking woman – and a librarian! – and...you're you! It seemed almost ridiculous that you would be interested in me!"

And yeah, that admission hurt.

When he didn't comment, she went on. "That night, I let Laney convince me to let my hair down. Literally. She picked out my clothes, did my makeup and...I was completely uncomfortable and I knew you were way out of my league. In my mind, I knew you would never be interested in someone like me – the *real* me – and I didn't handle things the right way and I'm sorry."

He simply stared at her.

"I don't know what I was thinking. Looking back now I know I should have been honest with you or just turned down your offer of a drink." She let out a breath and said, "It was childish and stupid and...I really am sorry."

And when he still didn't say anything, Shelby figured it would be best to just...throw in the towel.

"So, um...yeah. I guess I'll see you around," she said quietly and did her best to keep her head held high as she made her way back to her car. It was hard not to look back, but she didn't. Once she was at her car, she got in and kept her eyes forward and hated the way they stung with unshed tears.

On some level, she knew Sam would probably be annoyed – after all, she ran out on him. But that was the point she figured he'd focus on the most. Hearing how angry he was and the way he spoke to her only confirmed how she'd made the right decision. He was the kind of man she could admire from afar, but was way out of her league. She couldn't handle him when he was being charming, and she certainly couldn't handle him when he was angry.

Too bad there wasn't some sort of middle ground.

With a sad sigh, she started the car and went to back out of her spot when a white pickup truck blocked her in.

*Sam's* white pickup truck.

Shelby looked around wildly but stayed in her car as she watched Sam climb out and walk toward her. She wanted to bang her head on the steering wheel. Why couldn't he just let her leave with at least a little of her dignity? Hadn't she humiliated herself enough for one day?

With one hand over her rapidly-beating heart, she used the other to roll down the window.

"Can you get out of the car? Please?" he asked gruffly, and Shelby silently nodded. She climbed out and stood in front of him with the open door between them. Sam somehow managed to shift them so he could slam the car door and was instantly closer to her.

Her back was against the side of her Hyundai sedan as she held her breath and prepared for more criticism. She'd take it, too, because she knew she deserved it. She played a childish game with him and if she had to stand here and listen to him rant and rave some more, she'd deal with it.

And probably go home and cry afterwards.

"What are you doing right now?" he asked, his voice was so low and deep but at least it wasn't so full of disdain like it was minutes ago.

"I..." She stopped and cleared her throat and didn't meet his gaze. Instead, she was staring at the middle of his chest. "I was just going to pick up some Chinese food and go home and watch a movie."

*If he didn't think you were lame before, you just sealed the deal.*

Sam stared down at her. "Can I take you to dinner?"

Gasping softly, Shelby looked up and saw the small smile on his face. "You...you want to take me to dinner?"

His lips twitched slightly. "I believe that's what I just said."

"But...why?" Shelby knew if she were a guy and some chick was babbling like an idiot the way she was, she'd run in the opposite direction as fast as she could.

"Because I'd like to get to know you," he replied simply. "And now that I know we have something in common, I think we could have some great conversations." He paused. "Or should I say *more* great conversations."

She frowned. Great. This is what she inspired – conversation.

Awesome.

Letting out a breath, she said, "Yeah. Sure. That's fine."

Now it was Sam's turn to frown. "Did I say something wrong?"

This time, she wasn't going to explain it. She'd embarrassed herself enough for one day. "No. It's fine. Where should I meet you?" she asked with very little enthusiasm.

He was quiet for a moment as he considered her. "If you don't want to go, just say so, Shelby. I'm not going to force you to go out with me."

It wasn't so much that she didn't want to go – she was kind of curious about what it would be like to go out on a date with him – but considering who she was and his only observation about them was how they had a great conversation, she couldn't help but feel like it probably wasn't a good idea.

And she would be mortified if people saw them and openly questioned what someone like Sam was doing with someone like her.

"I'm just a little tired from the day and my knee kind of hurts from the fall," she said, knowing it wasn't a total lie. "If you'd like to grab some takeout with me, we can hang out at my place and talk." She shrugged. "No big deal."

His eyes narrowed at her. "Is that what you want to do?"

Swallowing hard, she nodded and was surprised when Sam seemed to relax again.

"Okay, let me have your order and your address and I'll meet you there in about thirty minutes." Then he paused and looked down at himself. "Make it an hour so I can at least run home to shower and change." He motioned to his dirt-and-sweat-covered clothes. "I don't have the cleanest job in the world."

Shelby wasn't exactly sure how to respond so she simply smiled and nodded.

"Will that be okay or are you starving?" he asked.

"No...no, I'm not starving and I can totally wait. Don't rush on my account." Forcing a smile, she was surprised when he opened the car door for her. He took out his phone and quickly tapped out her address and order and she was fascinated by his hands.

*Stop staring at him, you weirdo!*

With a smile, he confirmed – again – that he'd see her soon, Shelby sat in her car and watched him drive away.

And resigned herself to the fact that he could very well stand her up.

And it was no more than she deserved.

4

"You're here."

Sam had to grin at the surprise in Shelby's voice – like she didn't believe he had actually shown up with dinner.

"I said I would be."

"I...I know...I guess I just thought..."

"As hungry as I am, I don't think I could eat all of this by myself." He held up the bag of takeout.

She still didn't step aside to let him in and Sam took a moment to really study her. Earlier, he had been so shocked and angry that he hadn't appreciated how she looked. Even with her hair pulled back in a severe ponytail and wearing very little makeup, she still looked beautiful to him. The glasses she had on earlier looked good too and he wondered if she needed them all the time or if they were just for when she was working.

His eyes raked over her body and even in her practical black skirt and beige sweater set, he could see a hint of the curves beneath. Was she seriously trying to hide them and, if so...why?

Tilting his head toward her, he asked, "Mind if I come in? I think our dinner's getting cold."

That seemed to work, because she quickly stammered an apology and stepped aside. He followed her into her kitchen and had to admit, her place was really nice. It was small – it would best be described as a bungalow – but it was decorated in all beach tones and not overly feminine. He recognized several of the pieces from Mallory's shop.

"I see you're a shopper at my sister's place," he commented as he placed their dinner on the table.

"What?" she asked and then realized what he said. "Oh...yeah. I love her store! I've shopped there my whole life while Miss Barb owned it, but Mallory has really added some great items and I find myself shopping way more than I need to lately."

Laughing softly, he said, "And I'm sure Mallory appreciates it."

They worked together to set the table and they were about to sit when Shelby mumbled something under her breath and started to walk out of the room. He followed her and found her rummaging through a cabinet in her living room.

"Everything okay?"

"I was looking to see if I had any wine or any kind of alcohol to offer you, but...it doesn't look like I do. I'm not a big drinker or anything, and I'm sure you usually drink something stronger than water with your meals." She groaned. "I should have stopped and picked up something on the way home. Sorry." As she stood, he could see the disappointment on her face.

"It's all right, Shelby," he said, walking over and taking her by the hand before leading her back to the table. "I'm fine with a soda or sweet tea, if you have some."

That seemed to relax her because she smiled and... damn. She had a fantastic smile. Her cheeks got a little rosy and her entire face lit up.

"Why don't you sit down and I'll go grab our drinks?" she suggested and Sam agreed. Five minutes later, they were both seated and divvying up the food.

"Thank you for picking up dinner," she said shyly.

"Are you kidding? Chinese takeout is my favorite. And Panda Garden has some of the best I've ever had."

"You mean here in Magnolia?"

He shook his head. "Anywhere. Back home...well, I grew up in New York, but I've been living in Virginia for the last four years...there are places that are good, but not like this."

"I know what you mean. There are several places here that are really good, but I think I'm just biased." Pausing, she took another bite of her food before continuing. "As I'm sure you noticed, there were a lot of places that had damage from the hurricane and had to shut down, but they're all slowly starting to reopen."

Nodding, he agreed. "I will say this, we could use a good pizza place around here. Back in Virginia there are a few that were good but they don't even compare to the places I grew up around in New York." He grinned. "Now there was a city with a ton of great places to eat. I still miss it."

Shelby gave a small shrug and looked like she was just pushing her food around her plate now. "I haven't traveled much, but any time we do, I always miss the food from home." She shook her head and laughed softly. "I must sound pretty boring to you."

His forked clanked loudly on his plate. "Why do you keep doing that?"

She looked at him oddly. "Doing what?"

"Putting yourself down," he said and cringed at how loud he got. Letting out a long breath, he reached across the table and took one of her hands in his. "Look, it's obvious we've led different lives and it's not a bad thing! It's okay for us to be different and have different experiences and I'm not saying that one is better than the other!" Sam had to take a moment and calm down because her eyes were going wider with each word he spoke. Sighing softly, he said, "I know we don't know each other very well, but I'm hoping to change that. I want to get to know you, Shelby, but I will tell you this – what I do know about you, I really like. I hate hearing you talk negatively about yourself."

Her hazel eyes blinked at him and Sam could see tears forming and it just about gutted him. He squeezed her hand and then brought it to his lips and kissed it.

"The girl you met at the bar...well...that really isn't who I am," she said quietly, gently pulling her hand from his. "I think it's only fair that you know that. Call it false bravado or...whatever, but I really wasn't myself that night."

"So...you don't like Malibu cocktails?"

She looked at him oddly again. "No, I do."

"And...you don't like to dance?"

A shy smile crossed her face. "I like that too."

Nodding, he went on. "And I suppose you don't enjoy going out on your boat on a sunny day?"

"I appreciate what you're trying to do, Sam, but I'm being serious here."

"So am I," he countered. "Can we maybe start over? Pretend like we just met today? Like, I'm the knight in shining armor who saved you when you fell?"

Hanging her head, she laughed. "I was hoping you'd forget about that part – about what a klutz I am."

He noticed how she reached under the table to rub her knee. This time he reached out and tucked a finger under her chin and gently forced her to look up at him. Part of it was because he wanted to see her face when he said what he had to say, and the other was because he couldn't resist touching her.

"You're doing it again," he said, his voice low and firm. "No more of that tonight." Shelby gave a slight nod and they went back to their meals. "So, what do you do at the library?" he asked.

"I'm the head librarian," she replied, smiling.

"How long have you been there?"

"Sam, you really don't want to talk about that, do you? Compared to what you do..."

Sighing loudly, he replied, "Shelby, I really don't want to spend the night sounding like a broken record, okay? I asked because I do want to talk about it! I'm genuinely curious about what you do so could you just...please... answer the question?" He paused. "So...how long have you worked at the library?"

And she finally seemed to understand that he was being sincere because – once again – she relaxed and a serene smile crossed her face.

"Oh, my goodness, I've been working at the library since I was a freshman in high school. I started out volunteering, but I just fell in love with it. I'm an avid reader and love recommending books to people. It's not a glamorous job, but I can honestly say I love it. I enjoy going to work every day."

"Wow. Not too many people can say that."

She nodded. "I know. I am very blessed."

"I enjoy what I do – I've always liked working in the garden and making things grow – but...I can't say that I love what I'm doing right now."

"How come?"

He shrugged. "I think it's because of the terms of my great-grandfather's will. It was forced on me and there were rules and stipulations and...I don't know...it took some of the joy out of it for me."

"What kind of rules?"

"I have to work the company and run it for a year," he said and heard just how disgruntled he sounded. "I had a job, a life, back in Virginia that I had to walk away from to come and live here for a year."

"And what happens when that time is up? Will you go back to Virginia?"

He shrugged again and pushed his shrimp with lobster sauce around on the plate. "That's the plan. At that point I can legally sell the business."

"What happens if you leave before then?"

"Then the whole thing goes to my cousin Mason and I'm not allowed to profit from it at all."

"Wow."

"Yeah. I know. It was a crazy thing for Pops to put in there, but I think he knew I'd sell it and run." He shook his head. "Still, I would have liked to have the option. Now I feel like I'm here under protest."

Shelby went quiet for a moment. "I'm sure you must miss your life back in Virginia – your job, your friends, and..."

He knew exactly where she was going. "I wasn't involved with anyone, Shelby. Contrary to popular belief around here, I wouldn't be here with you if I had a girl-friend someplace else. And I'm not a kid. Virginia isn't that far away. If I were involved with someone, it wouldn't be completely impossible to do the long-distance thing."

It seemed like she didn't have a response to that so she

simply went back to her meal. But it bothered him how she even thought such a thing about him.

"Can I ask you something?" he asked with a bit of a snap to his voice. Putting his fork down, Sam pushed his plate aside and rested his arms on the table.

"Sure."

"If you have this...opinion of me...like I'm the type of guy who isn't faithful or that all I do is play around and go from woman to woman, why did you even sit with me that night? All you had to do was turn down my offer for a drink."

Her eyes went wide and she paled – like, visibly paled. He wanted to feel bad for being so blunt and putting her on the spot like that, but he was genuinely curious about why someone as seemingly shy as Shelby would even want to hang out with him.

Shelby mimicked his move, slid her plate away and gently wiped her mouth with her napkin before refolding it and putting it back down. Sam knew it was probably a delay tactic so she could come up with a good reason, but it was starting to annoy him.

"Shelby?"

"I don't know how to answer that without possibly insulting you."

Okay, he could appreciate her honesty. "It's all right. I'm used to it."

Her expression saddened and her shoulders slouched. "It's not all right, Sam. Just a few minutes ago you were lecturing me about not putting myself down. Well...I don't like to hear about people insulting you and I'm certainly not okay with being one of them!"

He had to admit, he liked it when she got a little feisty.

"Shelby, I know I have a reputation. When I was

younger, I was proud of it. It was fun, and I did whatever it was that I wanted without giving a damn about anyone else." He paused. "But I'm older now and I'm not the same person. At least...most of the time I'm not." With a wink, he reached out and took her hand in his again. "So, come on. Tell me."

"Honestly? I like to believe that there's more to people than the rumors and the preconceived notions you hear about. I've known who you are for years and I've heard a lot of stories – most of which weren't in very good taste. However, like you just said, I attributed a lot of it to being young and immature and...stupid. As a grown man, I figured there was a possibility that you had grown up and perhaps outgrown some of your wild ways." Then she paused and gave him a smile that was sweet and sexy. "And then part of me hoped you hadn't and I'd get to experience first-hand what it was like to be with wild Sam Westbrook."

Sam felt like his jaw must have hit the floor.

*Wow.*

He wasn't sure if he should be offended or flattered.

"Are you always this straight-forward or is it just with me?"

Her smile faded slightly. "You asked for honesty, Sam."

And then he couldn't help it, he laughed. "I know, but... I guess I wasn't quite expecting you to take it so literally. You didn't candy-coat that even a little bit, did you?"

She shook her head. "Didn't see the point."

"What's that supposed to mean?"

For a minute she didn't say a word.

Then her honesty was back in full force.

"I don't see the point in lying to you. I think we're both here tonight because of our unfortunate meeting. It's a Friday night and I'm sure there are dozens of places you'd rather be than here. This is nothing more than you putting your conscience to rest because you felt bad for me." She shrugged. "So while I appreciate the dinner and the conversation, I don't have any delusions about where this is going so I'm free to speak my mind."

Sam sputtered and choked and couldn't believe the things she was saying and yet...coming from Shelby, he wasn't surprised. When he finally calmed down, he rose and began clearing the dinner dishes. She jumped up to help him.

"You don't have to do that," she said. But when she went to take the dishes from his hand, Sam held firm. "I'm serious, Sam. It's not necessary."

He walked past her and cleared the plates, rinsed them, and then loaded them in her dishwasher. They worked together in silence until everything was cleared away. Facing her, he leaned against the kitchen counter, crossing his arms over his chest. No doubt she was thinking he was cleaning up so he could leave.

Wrong!

When she finished wiping down the table, she thanked him for dinner and started to walk to the front door. He followed, but once they were there, he asked, "So what kind of movie do you want to watch? A comedy? Drama? Action flick? Have you ever seen *Guardians of the Galaxy*?"

Wide-eyed again – something he found incredibly adorable on her – she stammered, "I...um...I guess...what? I thought you were leaving!"

Sam leaned in until they were nose to nose. "Nope." Then he placed a quick kiss there, walked into the living room and sat down on her sofa. "So? What are we watching?"

A little over two hours later, they watched the credits roll on *Guardians of the Galaxy* and Shelby had to admit it was a good movie. It certainly hadn't ever been on her radar, but she was glad she'd kept an open mind and watched it.

Sam had sat on the end of the couch and as the movie played on, he did his best to draw her closer and closer and now she was pressed against his side. "Did you like it?" he asked, a hint of excitement in his voice.

"I did! It wasn't quite what I was expecting, but I really enjoyed it!"

"There's a second one," he said casually. "You know...if you're interested. We could watch it right now and have a marathon."

Shelby considered that for a moment. It was still kind of early – barely nine o'clock. "Are you sure?" The question was out before she could stop it and when his expression fell a little, she felt bad. "I mean...maybe we should get some ice cream or at least some snacks before we sit through another two-hour movie."

*Good save, Shelby. Good save.*

Sam instantly relaxed and his smile was back. "Yeah, that sounds good. Do you have any ice cream here or should we go up to Sprinkles and get some sundaes?"

While Sprinkles was her favorite place for ice cream, Shelby also had quite a variety of her own in her freezer.

Hey, ice cream was one of the four food groups in her mind and it was incredibly important to always have some on hand.

Standing, she did her best to sound like she wasn't a nervous wreck at still having Sam here and said, "Oh, um...I think I have some inside. Why don't we go and see if there's anything we can work with?"

He stood and was right in front of her. Before she could register what was about to happen, Sam's head lowered and he kissed her softly on the lips. When he straightened, Shelby had to remind herself to breathe. "What...what was that for?"

One strong hand caressed her cheek. "That was for letting me join you for dinner and asking me to stay for dessert." His hand stilled. "And also because I've been wanting to do it since you opened the door earlier."

"Oh." Was it stupid that his words had her heart skipping like mad in her chest?

As if sensing her inner turmoil, Sam took her by the hand and led her into the kitchen. It took all of three minutes before he was laughing.

"What's so funny?"

"Anything we can work with?" he repeated her words back to her with a snort of laughter. "Shelby, you could rival Sprinkles with your variety of ice cream and toppings!"

She wanted to be mad, but...he had a point. "I hosted our book club last week and it was my friend Shari's birthday so we decided to have birthday sundaes rather than cake or cupcakes."

He looked at her skeptically. "So you never keep this kind of stuff on hand just for yourself?"

"Okay, fine. I enjoy ice cream. Sue me."

"A girl after my own heart," he said as he gave her a quick hug. "What's your favorite?"

On the kitchen counter were containers of chocolate, cookies and cream, butter pecan, strawberry, chocolate chip, mint chocolate chip, and chocolate chip cookie dough. "If it has chocolate in it, it's my favorite," she replied, laughing.

"The strawberry and butter pecan were left over from book club."

Sam grabbed the butter pecan and said, "Then it's a good thing I'm here to finish it off."

They worked side by side making their dessert. Shelby pulled out all kinds of toppings and she didn't bother being shy about what she prepared. This was probably going to be their one and only date before she was firmly placed in the friend-zone, so why pretend that she didn't enjoy eating?

*But he did kiss me...*

It didn't have to mean anything, right? She was sure guys like Sam did that sort of thing all the time. It would be silly to get her hopes up over one small kiss.

Once her sundae was ready, she excused herself to go get changed. She was still in her work clothes – except for her shoes – and if she was going to sit through another two-hour movie and eat ice cream, she really wanted to be comfortable.

When she walked out into the living room five minutes later wearing a pair of black leggings and a pink sweatshirt, Sam had their dessert waiting on the coffee table and he had cleaned up her kitchen.

It was more than some of her actual friends usually did.

Sitting down beside him, she reached for her bowl. "Ready?"

He was staring at her. "Where are your glasses?"

Oh, right...

Feeling a bit foolish, she explained about why she wore them and by the time she was done she was more than ready for him to tell her she was crazy.

But he didn't.

"You look good with them," he said instead. Then he

leaned in a little closer. "But you look just as good without them. Plus, now I can see those beautiful eyes."

*Oh my...*

"So, um...ready for part two?" she asked, knowing she was blushing from head to toe from his compliment.

Nodding, Sam hit the play button on the remote before picking up his sundae. "I have to say, I'm impressed."

Shelby had the spoon halfway to her mouth when she paused. "Why?"

"I was expecting you to make yourself a dainty little bowl of ice cream." He nodded toward her bowl. "But the marshmallow, hot fudge, whipped cream, and sprinkles totally proved me wrong. So...I'm impressed."

She gave him a quick smile because she wasn't sure what else she should do and took a spoonful as the movie began.

"Mallory does the same thing with her desserts. She may eat like a bird all day but if there is ice cream around, she puts everything in the bowl but the kitchen sink."

Well, it was nice to know she had something in common with his sister and that he found it endearing.

Tugging her a little bit closer, Sam winked at her as they settled in to watch the movie.

And two hours later, she was full and a little sleepy. Sam had taken their bowls into the kitchen earlier after they finished eating and now she was curled up next to him with her head once again on his shoulder. Her eyes were fighting to stay open, but Shelby knew it wouldn't be long before she was out.

Forcing herself to move, she yawned.

"Uh-oh, is this your subtle way of saying you didn't enjoy the movie?"

"What? Oh...no. No, that's not it at all. It was good, but I think I liked the first one better," she admitted.

"Yeah, I feel the same way. It's still a great franchise," he said, studying her. "Are you tired then? Do you want me to go?"

Really, she didn't. It had been a nice evening and maybe if she prolonged it a little bit she wouldn't feel quite so bad about them not getting involved romantically.

*He did kiss you earlier.*

Oh, yeah. That.

But he hadn't made a single move since the kiss, other than keeping her close while they watched the movies. It didn't mean anything, did it? Maybe he just liked having her sit close to him. Maybe that was his thing.

She was so bad at figuring men out, she thought miserably.

"I want to say no, but..." She yawned again. "Sorry."

"It's okay, Shelby." Standing up, Sam reached down for her hand and gently pulled her to her feet. "Can I see you tomorrow?"

Frowning, she looked up at him. "You mean to hang out again?"

His dark eyes blinked at her several times as if not understanding her question. "Um...I was hoping to take you out properly – dinner and whatever else it is you might like to do. Other than sailing, you never really answered my question that night."

Taking a step back, now it was Shelby who didn't seem to get it. "Why do you want to take me to dinner? We...we hung out tonight and...there's no hard feelings. I mean, I'm still sorry for not being honest with you the night we met, but...don't feel like you need to keep hanging out with me."

The fierce look from earlier was back as he took a step

toward her. "Are we back to that again? Why exactly do you think I'm here, Shelby?" he asked, frustration practically bristling off of him.

"I...like I said...I figured we were just hanging out to... you know...talk things out. And we have." Hopefully he couldn't see her slight tremble. She wasn't used to someone questioning her like this.

But then again, she wasn't used to dealing with anyone quite like Sam.

He took another step toward her. "Is that why you agreed to let me come over? Because you needed to clear your conscience? Or thought that I needed to?"

"Um...I don't know. Maybe."

Another step toward her. "You want to know why I'm here?" He didn't wait for her to respond. "I'm here because for two damn weeks you've been all I can think about. Seeing you earlier in the library parking lot had me feeling like I won the damn lottery – like I was getting a second chance with you!" Another step and now he towered over her. "But more than anything, I'm here because you're someone I want to know better, dammit!"

"Sam, I..."

"But if that's not what you want – if I'm not someone you want to know – then say something right now, Shelby," he demanded. "Right now, before my feelings grow even deeper. Because believe it or not, what I felt for you that night at the bar is nothing compared to how I feel right now."

She gasped softly and her foolish heart began its wild dance again. Swallowing hard, she looked up at him – saw the sincerity and the anguish in those dark depths. "I..." She paused and collected her thoughts which were going a million miles a minute in her head. "How do you feel?"

It was something she needed to know. It was one thing if he was casually interested in her – which was what she expected him to say. But what if it were more? What if it were something deep and warm and wonderful and scary and everything she was feeling too?

Reaching out, Sam cupped her face in his hands and rested his forehead against hers. "I feel like you're someone I need to know."

His voice was low and gruff and rumbly enough that she felt it all the way down to her toes.

How could she possibly explain to him that she was too afraid to believe him? That she didn't have the confidence in herself to believe him?

As if sensing her thoughts, he quietly said, "You've been brutally honest with me all night, Shelby. Don't stop now. Tell me what you're thinking."

There really was something about Sam that made her feel like she could say anything – even if she shouldn't.

"I guess I'm afraid to believe that you really want to get to know me," she admitted softly. "I'm nothing special, Sam. I'm not the type of girl you usually…"

He placed one finger across her lips to stop her flow of words. "Please don't keep throwing that back in my face." He closed his eyes as if in pain. "I know I've done a lot of stupid things and I've made a lot of bad choices, but that has nothing to do with you and me. When I saw you that night, all I remember thinking was…finally, there she is."

Her eyes went wide at the intensity of his words. No one had ever said anything like that to her before. She wasn't the kind of girl or woman who caused that kind of reaction – she knew that and she was okay with it. But after seeing the look on Sam's face as he spoke, Shelby knew she had to have more – needed to see where this went and what would come from an admission like his.

"Wow," she whispered, because it's all she could force herself to say.

The smile Sam gave her was one of sweet relief. Unable to help herself, she placed her hand on his chest, and, feeling his rapid heartbeat, she grew bold. Her hand smoothed up and over his shoulder and then raked up into his hair. Up on her tiptoes, she pressed her lips to his and prayed she wouldn't panic or freak out again.

When his arms slowly banded around her waist, Shelby knew this time was different. He was being cautious and careful and, undoubtedly, holding back so he didn't spook her. The kiss was chaste – slow and sweet. Only this time, she was the one to seek more. Her tongue tentatively reached out and skimmed along his bottom lip and she heard his sharp intake of breath. It made her bold. Pressing herself more firmly against him, she reveled in the feel of his warm, hard body. And when he maneuvered them back over the sofa, she felt her excitement grow.

Sam sat and gently guided Shelby down so he could cradle her in his lap and, if anything, she thought it was the perfect position for them. His arms were around her, holding her securely to him, all the while their kiss just continued. There wasn't the same intensity as there was the night they met, and that was more than okay with her. She was enjoying this – the way they were slowly getting acquainted with each another.

Squirming slightly against him, she gulped for air when Sam broke the kiss and gazed at her face. His breath was coming just as raggedly as hers and she wished more than anything that she didn't need oxygen quite so much because she already missed the feel of his mouth on hers.

One of his hands came up and took the clip out of her hair. She let out a small moan of pleasure because it had been bothering her all night, but when that same hand anchored up into her hair and began massaging her scalp, it felt like she had died and gone to heaven.

*Good lord, if a three-second scalp massage feels this good, what would sex with him be like?*

Hopefully she'd find out.

Diving in for another kiss, Shelby was pleasantly surprised that Sam seemed just as anxious as she was for another taste. She twisted and turned in his lap until she was straddling him and it was like she didn't even recognize herself. She wasn't normally this forward or – dare she say, aggressive? – but there was no way for her to fight what she was feeling. For two weeks she had kicked herself every day for running like she did and now that she was getting a second chance, she was taking it.

With everything she had, apparently.

They kissed, they rolled over and stretched out on the sofa until Sam was on top of her and Shelby wrapped herself completely around him. So many times she thought to break their kiss and simply ask him to stay – to move things into the bedroom – but his hands and mouth kept distracting her until she didn't know her own name, let alone where they were half the time.

At some point – it could have been minutes later, it could have been hours – Sam raised his head and smiled down at her. He was so handsome, so sexy, so...everything she ever fantasized about...and he was here with her.

"Shelby," he said, low and thick. "Damn."

Yeah. She knew exactly what he meant.

Her hand smoothed up his back and up into his hair in hopes of guiding his mouth back to hers, but...he moved.

He stood.

She stayed where she was on the sofa and looked up at him in confusion.

"I should go," he said after a long moment.

"Go?"

He nodded. "Dinner tomorrow night, right?"

He was leaving? Now? Seriously?

"Um..."

Doing a move that was clearly becoming his thing, Sam reached for her hand and gently pulled her to her feet. He kissed her one last time on the lips before letting out a low growl. Clearing his throat, he said, "You know how badly I want to stay, right?"

Shelby nodded and wanted to say she felt the same, but she couldn't seem to make her voice work.

He hugged her tight. "But I don't think it's the right thing to do," he said, and her only consolation was that he sounded as miserable about it as she felt. "Let me take you out tomorrow." He pulled back and studied her face. "I want to do this right. I feel like I came on too strong that night and...and I'm not willing to do anything that you might regret."

Well, damn. He was sweet, sexy, funny, *and* considerate? How was she supposed to resist?

"That night...that was my own issue, Sam. It wasn't about you. Not really. I want you to know that."

With a lopsided grin, he pulled her back into his embrace. "Thank you for saying that."

"It's the truth."

Slowly they broke apart and walked over to the front door. He opened it and kissed her one more time. "You are pure temptation. You know that, right?"

Blushing, she shook her head.

"It's true." Tucking a finger under her chin, his expression turned serious. "Thank you for inviting me over and for giving me another chance. I'll pick you up tomorrow at seven. Will that work?" He reached into his pocket and pulled out his phone so they could exchange numbers. Once that was done, he kissed her one last time and walked out the door.

And Shelby swore part of her heart went with him.

5

A WEEK LATER, Sam walked backwards down the walkway in front of Shelby's house and waved as she closed the door. It was late – almost two in the morning – and yet he'd never felt so awake and alive and...happy.

Yeah, that last one came as a bit of a shock because it had been quite some time since he'd felt it.

He and Shelby had spent every day together this week and never did more than share heated kisses on her couch.

And yeah, that one came as a shock to him too because he was a sophomore in high school the last time he'd ever done anything so chaste.

Every night they were together, he felt like it could be the right time to simply scoop her up in his arms and take her to bed, and yet...he hadn't. Why? That was the million-dollar question. And as he climbed into the car, Sam refused to acknowledge what could possibly be the answer.

Fear.

Yeah, big bad Sam Westbrook was afraid to take Shelby to bed.

She wasn't a virgin – a fact she volunteered one night

when things really seemed like they were heading to her bedroom – but she was almost as sweet and innocent as one.

For all his wild ways, Sam never found himself attracted to someone like Shelby before. He preferred his women to be a little more worldly – the kind who weren't looking for anything more than a good time.

And preferably nothing more beyond a single night.

Shelby was the complete opposite of that and rather than that being a turnoff, he found it incredibly attractive. The more he got to know her, the more he wanted to know. And whenever the thought of sex with her came to mind, it made him realize how he wanted things to be different with her.

Then he'd get into his own head and freak himself out and leave.

He was beginning to understand why she ran that first night.

Tomorrow they were going to go out on her boat with a picnic lunch. She had mentioned it to him earlier tonight and he could tell by the look on her face that she was hoping to make it a romantic outing.

Did he really want them to make love for the first time out on her boat in the middle of the Sound?

*There were worse places...*

And he should know.

He was usually the king of finding them.

Climbing into his truck, he muttered a curse. She was too good for him. What right did he have to keep pursuing her? At the end of the day, he wasn't staying here in Magnolia and she deserved someone better than him. Shelby deserved the kind of man who didn't have so much baggage and issues and a bad reputation.

But damn if he could give her up.

As he drove through town, a few other thoughts came to mind – like how he was beginning to see a different side to the people of Magnolia. Don't get him wrong, there were plenty of people who looked at them like they were an oddity and there were even a couple of not-so-subtle whispers of "What's a girl like Shelby doing with him?" but for the most part, he had been enjoying their interaction around town.

Last night they had gone to pick up pizza and Sal – the owner's father who was notorious for flirting with all the girls in town – came out, clapped Sam on the back while smiling at Shelby, and said, "You've got a good one here, Shelby! You treat him right!"

Never before had Sam felt like blushing but right then and there, he had. And what was even more amazing was how the other patrons waiting for their pizzas didn't try to correct Sal and there wasn't one whisper of disbelief.

One business down, only another two dozen or so to go, he thought.

The drive home didn't take long and when he turned off the engine, he thought his eyes were playing tricks on him.

Colton was just leaving.

That would mean...

"Oh hell no," he muttered, a sick feeling threatening to overwhelm him.

His mother was having sex? Seriously? And with Colton?

The thought of having *that* conversation right now was beyond unappealing, so Sam sank down in the driver's seat and waited until Colton pulled away.

And even then he stayed put for a solid five minutes before heading into the house.

Once there, he tiptoed into the kitchen and grabbed a

bottle of water. The house was dark and sort of like walking through a minefield with all the construction mess going on in every room, but he was learning how to make his way around without hurting himself.

However, turning around and running into his mother had him screaming out as if in pain.

"Geez, Mom! A little warning next time!"

Susannah Coleman clutched the front of her robe and looked up at her son with wide eyes. "What are you doing up, Sam? Or...here. Or...I thought you were out for the night!"

"I was out, but now I'm home," he stated. "Why? Am I not allowed to come home?"

"No, I just meant...I mean you usually..." She sighed and walked past him to grab a bottle of water for herself. She took a long sip before facing him again. "When did you get home?"

"Right before Colton slunk out of here," he said with a little more heat than was necessary.

And judging by his mother's face, she shared that opinion.

"Sorry," he murmured.

"No, no. I think we should talk about this," Susannah said, walking over to the kitchen table and sitting down. She pushed out a chair for Sam and waited.

It would be childish to try to be defiant, so he went and sat down.

"Well?" she asked.

"Well, what?"

"I thought you wanted to talk about this."

"Me? You were the one who just said you thought we should talk," he said, unable to meet her eyes.

Laughing softly, Susannah nodded. "Okay, that's true.

Sorry. I'm a little sleepy and I guess I'm not thinking straight."

"Mom, we really don't need to do this right now. It's not a big deal."

"Really?" she deadpanned. "Because your comment about Colton made it seem like it was a big deal."

Sam let out a long breath and slouched down in his chair. "Okay, fine. I didn't realize you and Colton were...you know..."

"Dating?"

Now he looked at her. "Seriously? That's what you want to call it?"

"That's what it is," she countered. "Colton and I are dating and we've...taken things to the next level." She paused. "I had forgotten how wonderful it was to be intimate with a man and Colton has been...well...we've been dating for a while now and..."

"Ugh...Mom, please."

"When did you become such a prude?" she teased. "I would expect your sister to react like this, Sam, but not you."

"Yeah, well...you'll have to excuse me for not wanting to sit around talking about my mother's sex life." He shuddered for dramatic effect.

"I'll admit it's not my favorite way to pass the time either, but considering we're both living here, I think we need to talk about it. Not specifics," she quickly corrected, "but the fact that Colton is going to be coming around and... there may come a time when I don't ask him to go home at two in the morning."

If only he had stayed at Shelby's a little bit longer...

"And just so you know," Susannah went on, "if you ever wanted to bring a girl home, I...well...I wouldn't stop you.

You're a grown man and this is your home too, so...just know I'm okay with it."

He stared at her for a long moment. "Uh...thanks. I guess."

Seeming to relax, Susannah let out a small sigh. "So where were you and Mason at tonight? One of the local bars?"

"No," he said. "I, uh...I didn't go out with Mason tonight."

She looked at him curiously. "Oh. I just thought..."

Hell, they were already having the world's most awkward conversation, he might as well add to it. "I'm sort of seeing someone."

Her eyes went wide and a small smile crossed her face. "Really?"

He nodded.

"Is it serious?"

As much as Sam thought it was, it felt like it was too soon to admit that to anyone who wasn't Shelby. "It's only been a week."

And then her smile faded and she seemed disappointed. "Oh."

"Oh? What does that mean?"

She shrugged. "I was hoping for something a little more encouraging from you than 'It's only been a week.'"

Okay, maybe it wasn't the worst idea to talk to his mother about this...

"I actually met her three weeks ago," he began. "We met at a club in Wilmington and...she left before I could get her number or even her last name. Then I ran into her here in town a week ago and we've been hanging out together every night since."

And her smile was back. "Well that sounds lovely," she

said sleepily right before she yawned. Standing, she looked down at him. "Will I get to meet her sometime?"

Standing up beside her, he said, "Yeah. Sure." Wrapping an arm around her, he led them out of the kitchen. "Let's just hope it doesn't happen at two in the morning when we all come down here to grab a drink."

Susannah laughed softly even as she pinched him playfully. "Do *not* even put that image in my head," she said. "As much as I said I don't mind you having an overnight guest, that doesn't mean I want to hang out with both of you after...well...you know."

"Ditto, Mom. I actually hid in my car until Colton pulled away. I did *not* want to have a conversation with him right then and there."

That had her laughing again. "Oh, lord. What a pair we are, huh? I swear, I never thought this would be my life." She shook her head. "I avoided dating for so many years and I thought that was it for me. If anyone would have told me I could find a decent man at my age..."

"Mom, you're not ancient, you know. You're not even fifty, for crying out loud. And if Colton makes you happy, then...then I'm happy too. Even if the whole thing feels weird right now."

They continued to walk up the stairs. "I'm sorry you feel that way. I guess I didn't think I needed to discuss it with you or Mallory." She looked up at him when they reached the landing. "This is all new to me too, you know."

"I know, Mom, and I wasn't saying it to be rude or disrespectful. I was just being honest."

"Well, if it makes you feel any better, it feels weird sometimes when you and Mallory date anyone."

He chuckled. "Really? Why?"

"Because you're my babies," she explained. "I know this

is the way life goes and you were going to grow up and get involved with people, have sex…"

"Mom…"

"Oh, hush!" she teased. "I'm just saying how the reality of it sometimes is weird for a parent too. I had the hardest time looking Jake in the eye once I knew he and Mallory were dating."

"Tell me about it. Every once in a while I still get the urge to punch him."

"But you won't."

"Yeah, I won't."

"For all you know, Mallory may want to punch your girlfriend too."

His eyes went wide and it made him laugh again. "Mallory? No way. She would never do something like that. Besides, Shelby's bought quite a few things from the shop so Mallory wouldn't want to lose a customer."

Susannah took a step through the doorway to her bedroom before turning back to look at Sam. "Really? Does she know your sister? Are they friends?"

Sam shook his head and yawned. "I don't think so." He yawned again and then noticed his mother doing the same. "We'll talk about this another time. I'm beat."

"Does she live here in town? Your girlfriend?"

"Mom, we can talk about Shelby tomorrow, right?" He couldn't stop yawning and gave her a small wave as he made his way down the hall to his room."

"Wait…Shelby?" Susannah said, stepping out into the hall. "Shelby Abbott?"

Sam nodded but was too tired to turn around and keep the conversation going.

"You know she's…"

"Goodnight, Mom," he called over his shoulder. Whatever it was she had to say about Shelby could wait. Sleep couldn't.

———————

Sandwiches and salads? Check.

Brownies? Check.

Sweet tea and bottled water? Check and check.

Shelby looked around her kitchen as she began to pack her giant cooler bag and tried to see if she had forgotten anything. She had plates, cups, and utensils here in the bag along with the food and yet she still felt like she was missing something.

Then she remembered.

Condoms.

Yup. She had gone to the drugstore two towns over and purchased a box because she wanted to make sure she was completely prepared if she decided to seduce Sam while out on their sail today.

She was still up in the air on whether or not she could pull that off since she'd never seduced anyone in her entire life. It was something she usually left up to the men she dated. But with Sam...she wanted to. He made her feel sexy and confident and as much as she was enjoying their time together and seeing how hard it was for him to stay in control, she really wanted to watch him lose it too.

For her.

She had a feeling it was going to be very empowering to know she could seduce someone like Sam.

Quickly running to her bedroom, she grabbed the condoms and tucked them into the side pocket of the cooler bag. Once that was done, she zipped the bag closed and went back to her room to change into her bathing suit. It was unseasonably warm out – not warm enough to swim – but she always wore a bathing suit under her clothes when on the boat.

Only...this time that bathing suit happened to be a bikini.

With conservative parents, Shelby had always been taught to dress modestly and that meant wearing one-piece bathing suits. It was something that never really bothered her and as much as she was sometimes envious of the girls in the bikinis, she had been fine with who she was.

But again, she wanted to be sexy for Sam. She wanted him to look at her and see her as a desirable woman and not the practical and boring one she clearly was.

Stripping down, she quickly slipped the bikini on and then turned to look at herself in the mirror and froze.

*This is not who I am...*

Did it look good on her? Yes.

Did it fit properly? Yes.

Was she comfortable in it? Heck no.

Muttering a curse, she took it off and pulled out one of her one-piece suits and then stared at her reflection and with a sigh thought, "This is me."

Well that was depressing. But still, better she not be distracted by how uncomfortable she was, right? She could still seduce Sam. She would just have to do it while wearing a boring and practical bathing suit.

"Ugh, can those two words just disappear from the English language?" she asked her reflection. Stepping away from the mirror, she slid on a pair of shorts and pulled on a sweatshirt before reaching for her tennis shoes.

And then completely avoided the mirror on her way out of the room.

With nothing left to do but wait, Shelby walked around

the house, fluffing pillows on the sofa and straightening knick-knacks before giving up and calling Laney. She needed a little pep talk before Sam arrived.

"Hey, Shell! What's up?"

"Not much. Just waiting for Sam to get here. We're going out on the boat today."

"Ooh...sailing! Good for you! Please tell me you're not wearing the navy blue one-piece."

*And add predictable to the words to describe me.*

"Um...yeah. I am," she said with a weary sigh. "I bought a bikini and I tried it on, but...I don't know. I was too self-conscious and knew it would distract me the entire time."

"And Sam too," Laney added with a laugh. "That's the point, Shell. You want him to be distracted! You need to embrace your inner goddess and let her out to play once in a while!"

They'd had this conversation multiple times over the last week alone, and yet Shelby still couldn't seem to do it. "I know I should, but...it felt weird! And I knew I would probably be some sort of babbling idiot because I was self-conscious about what I was wearing and it would ruin the day! Maybe next time..."

"What time is Sam coming over?"

"What?"

"When is Sam supposed to be there?" Laney demanded.

"I don't know...twenty minutes, I guess."

"Damn, not enough time."

"Time for what?"

"For me to come over and see you in the bikini so I can tell you how amazing you look!"

"It's not about how I look, Laney. It's about how I feel," she explained. "And honestly, I should not have to change who I am to please Sam or anyone! He's seen me – the real me – this whole last week. Why do I need to change that?"

"Okay, wow," Laney said quietly. "I had no idea you felt that way."

"Well, you should! We've been friends since forever and you've always told me to be true to myself, and this is who I am. I'm the girl in the one-piece bathing suit! The one too afraid to tell my parents I don't wear glasses anymore!"

"Yeah, we're still going to circle back to that one every once in a while..."

Shelby collapsed down on her sofa and sighed. "I'm a mess. I don't know why Sam keeps coming around. He could have any girl in town – or in any town for that matter. Why is he wasting time with me?"

"I'm going to pretend you didn't just say that," Laney said fiercely. "It shouldn't matter who Sam can have. The fact is he wants you! He's seen you at your best and at your worst and at everything in between and you know why he's still coming around? Because you're an amazing and incredible person! I hate when you put yourself down like that and it has to stop! As your best friend, I demand that it stop! What is it going to take for you to believe in yourself? You are Shelby-freaking-Abbott and you are a beautiful, awesome rock star!"

Shelby chuckled. "A rock star? You've heard me sing, right?"

"A metaphorical rock star," Laney corrected with a small laugh. "But I'm serious, Shell. You need to believe in yourself. And here's something else for you to think about – maybe there are people wondering why you're with someone like Sam."

"What? Why would anyone think that?"

"Really? How about because he's got a reputation for

being kind of a screw-up? Or how he's a serial dater who never gets into any kind of relationship beyond a night or two? Or that he's skating through life on the charity of his great-grandfather? These are all things people think, Shell, and when you compare that to the kind of person you are, he seems way beneath you. So the snobbery goes both ways."

"Wow."

"Yeah, I know."

"I never once looked at Sam like that," she said.

"And I guarantee he's never looked at you like you weren't enough for him."

"I'm still not wearing the bikini. Not today."

"I guess that's something."

Sighing, Shelby rested her head back against the sofa. "You want to know the strangest part of this whole thing?"

"Sure."

"Sam is nothing at all like I thought he'd be – and I know we just covered the whole not-passing-judgement thing – but even knowing his past, he's still treats me better than I can ever remember a guy treating me."

"Seriously? I find that hard to believe. You've dated a lot of very polite guys, Shell. How is that even possible?"

"It's hard to explain, but...he talks to me. Like really talks to me," she began. "We have these weird and random conversations that range from borderline ridiculous topics to super serious current events. And when I talk, he listens to me. So many guys I've dated just want to be the ones to talk or it's only their opinion that counts and...Sam's not like that. He makes me feel important." Then she sighed. "Maybe that sounds pathetic, but...there it is."

"It's not pathetic. It's really kind of cool and I'm more than a little envious. I can't remember the last time I had a genuine intelligent conversation with a guy. Normally it's all so superficial."

"Exactly! And we have so much more in common than I ever thought possible! My parents always tried to fix me up with guys they thought I had something in common with, but they were wrong. Just because I work in a library, doesn't necessarily mean I'm only interested in books! I mean, yes, books are a huge part of my life, but they're not everything."

"Don't let the patrons of the library hear you say that!" Laney teased. "They think you live, breathe, eat, and sleep books!"

It was true that Shelby had a vast knowledge of their catalog, but it wasn't her only interest or hobby. "They'll just have to deal with it," she said with a small laugh. "We both love sailing and eating Chinese food. We have similar taste in music, we both love playing word games like Scrabble or Bananagrams...he got me to watch a superhero movie and I got him interested in *The Crown*." She smiled at all the memories. "This feels like one of the healthiest relationships I've ever had and it's only been a week!"

"That's the honeymoon phase," Laney said a little more seriously. "Everyone feels like that in the first month or two of a relationship. After that, when you settle in and some of the newness fades, you start seeing the things you don't like or start finding things that get on your nerves."

"Yeah, I know. But I'm hoping it lasts longer than that before I start to think that way. If we can stay like this until he moves back to Virginia..."

"Wait, wait, wait...he's moving back to Virginia? When?"

*Probably not the best time to bring up that subject.*

"The other night we were talking and he mentioned

how the only reason why he moved here to Magnolia was because his great-grandfather left him the business."

"O-kay..."

"And he has to work it for a full year before he's allowed to sell it otherwise he forfeits everything having to do with it." She sighed. "If it were up to Sam, he would have sold it immediately and never come here except to visit his mother and sister."

"Well that sucks."

"Tell me about it."

"So...let me ask you this – if you know this is temporary, is it smart for you to be getting this involved with him?"

Another sigh. "There's another eight months or something like that before it happens and – if I'm allowed to be judgmental – I think his attention span will be long gone by then."

"You're putting yourself down again."

"No, I'm being...practical."

Dammit, she really hated that word! Why did it have to be so appropriate for her?

"Maybe he'll surprise you."

"To what end, Laney? This is my home! This is where I want to live and raise my own family. I love this town, I love the library...I'm not looking to travel the world or live someplace new."

"You don't know that, Shell. You've never even tried to live anyplace else!"

"I most certainly did! I lived in Illinois for four years for college!"

"Yeah, but...that's not the same."

"How is it not? I lived there, worked there, went to school there, made friends there...I had a life there, Laney!

And I've traveled around enough that I know where I'm comfortable and where I'm not."

"So you're telling me if at the end of this eight months, Sam asked you to move to Virginia with him because he loved you, you would say no?"

*Oh, god...could that really happen?*

"I don't think we need to worry about that. It's never going to happen."

"Never say never..."

"Trust me. If nothing else, I'm a realist."

"Shell..."

"I'm not saying that I don't think it's possible for Sam to have some serious feelings for me or even fall in love with me, but I don't think he's the kind of man who'll settle down either."

"You can't know that already and it's too soon to even be speculating about it, so...let's not go there. This discussion is bordering on depressing. Let's change the subject. Did you pack a cooler for the boat?"

Actually, Shelby was a little relieved to talk about something else. While she knew she said she was a realist, that didn't mean she wanted to deal with that particular reality right now. Today she wanted to be carefree and happy and bold and sexy – she wanted to be a woman who was going out for an afternoon sail with a very attractive man and hopefully do something she'd never done before.

The sound of a car door slamming outside had her looking toward the front door and smiling.

He was here.

It was time.

Sitting up, she did her best to sound casual. "Listen, Laney, I need to go. I think Sam just pulled up."

"Ooh...okay, have fun," she said excitedly. "And don't do anything I wouldn't do!"

"Does that include sex on a boat?" And even though she meant to sound like she was making a joke, her voice cracked a bit and gave her away.

"Girl, I seriously hope you do get to do that today and then I'm going to want all the details on Monday!"

"Not all the details, Laney! Sheesh!"

"Okay, just the PG-rated version then."

She shook her head even as she laughed. "I make no promises."

The doorbell rang and she jumped to her feet. "I have to go. Wish me luck!"

"You don't need luck. Just be yourself. I'll talk to you Monday!"

They hung up and Shelby tossed her phone onto the sofa and took several long, steadying breaths before she walked over to the door. Smoothing a hand over her shirt and then over her hair, she did her best to appear completely calm.

But as soon as she pulled the door open and saw Sam standing there in a pair of shorts, a t-shirt, and a boyish grin, a dozen butterflies took flight in her belly.

It was going to be a good day.

A really good day.

## 6

IT HAD DEFINITELY BEEN a good idea to come out and spend some time on the boat, Sam thought a few hours later. The sky was completely clear, the temperature was unseasonably warm for late March, and having Shelby to himself with no distractions was the icing on the cake.

Her boat was a bowrider – similar to the one his future brother-in-law had – but Shelby's was a little newer. When they had pulled up at the marina, he was a little surprised. When she said she liked to go sailing, he envisioned her having an actual sailboat, not a sporty motorized boat.

It was a pleasant surprise and he loved how she let him drive.

Spending his summers in Magnolia Sound had meant he learned how to sail at a young age. His cousin Mason had a boat of his own that they used to go out on frequently in the last several years, but Shelby's boat was the first he felt comfortable at behind the wheel. Looking over at her, he smiled. Her hair was up in a messy bun, she had on sunglasses, her head was thrown back and she was just enjoying the feel of the sun on her face.

She was breathtaking.

Yeah, he couldn't ever remember thinking that of a woman who was dressed as casually as Shelby currently was, but then again, there was nothing about their relationship that was usual for him. It didn't seem to matter what they were doing, he enjoyed it mainly because it was with her. He loved listening to her talk and hearing her great laugh, but most of all he loved how she accepted him for who he was.

Looking straight ahead, he tried to find a place where they could drop anchor for a little while and have some lunch. There wasn't a lot of traffic out on the water, but he still hoped to find a spot that wouldn't be in anyone's way. There weren't any secluded areas to dock and he knew no matter what, they were going to be on display somehow.

Out of the corner of his eye, he caught a flash of color and when he turned, he felt his heart kick hard in his chest.

Shelby had taken off her sweatshirt and revealed the skin-tight bathing suit she had on underneath.

His mouth went dry and he quickly maneuvered the boat a little closer to a wooded area and turned it off. Turning, he stared down at her and had to hide a smile as she looked around in confusion.

"We're stopping already? Are you hungry?"

And that was the best thing about Shelby – she was adorably naïve.

And he meant that in the nicest possible way.

There wasn't anything coy about her and her mind wasn't set on playing games. She was legitimately concerned about whether or not he was ready for lunch.

She climbed to her feet and stretched and Sam's mind instantly went where it shouldn't.

How the fabric clung to her.

How hard her nipples were.

It was torture not to reach out and touch her right now, but he was really trying not to pounce. Swallowing hard, he said, "I could eat."

She smiled brightly at him and immediately began setting up their food. There was a small area where a table folded out and within minutes, she had lunch spread out for them. Sam joined her and as they ate, they shared stories about their experiences out on different boats.

"I always love the Magnolia Boat Parade on Memorial Day weekend," she said with a look of pure bliss on her face. "Have you ever been here for that?"

Sam shook his head.

"It's amazing. There's one early in the day and the shore is lined with people waving...anyone can join the long line of boats and it's always a lot of fun waving to the little kids who are sitting on the dock waving their flags."

"Is there another one?"

She nodded. "After dark, there's another parade and the boats that sail through are decorated with twinkly lights – you know, like Christmas lights – all in red, white, and blue. So many people get creative and make a design out of the lights and you can't see what it is until after dark. You should really try to see it this year."

Unable to help himself, he grinned. "Know of a good spot I could scope out so I could watch?"

For a minute, she must not have understood what he was implying, but then a beautiful and shy smile crossed her face. "I might have a few suggestions." She paused. "But maybe I should show them to you myself."

Reaching across the table, he took one of her hands in his. "I wouldn't want to watch it any other way."

They ate in companionable silence for a few minutes

before continuing their conversation about their favorite type of boats. As much as he enjoyed a good sailboat, it was nice not to have to put in so much work on this trip. He was surprised when Shelby expressed the same thing.

"My father has a sailboat that he honestly adores," she said, "and we still go out on it as a family at least once a month when the weather is good, but I didn't want something like that. He got me a great deal on this boat and it's the perfect size for me."

"Someday I hope to have a boat of my own, but it's never been a big priority," he admitted. "I get my sailing fix in while I'm here in the summer – or at least, that's the way it was when I was growing up. Now I know whenever I come home to visit, there's always going to be at least one that I can use if the urge hits."

She nodded but her smile faded a bit.

Tilting his head, he considered her. What did he say wrong?

"You're counting down the days until you can go back to Virginia, I'm sure," she said casually and that's when it hit him.

He wasn't.

Not anymore.

Reaching across the table, he took one of her hands in his and clasped it firmly. "If you had asked me that a month ago I would have said yes. Hell, if you had asked me three weeks ago, I would have said it." He paused and looked down at their hands. "But I haven't even thought about my life back there since we met." Now his eyes met hers and he saw the stunned look on her face. "I don't know what the future is going to bring, Shelby. I can't give you any kind of guarantee. All I know is that right now, my life and everything I want is right here."

"Sam..."

"It's true," he said. "I have a calendar in my room that I was crossing off the days on before we met. I haven't even looked at it since that night. That's not my focus right now. I think for the last several months, I was so focused on all the reasons I wanted to leave because there wasn't a reason for me to stay."

"Your family is here," she reminded him quietly.

As much as Sam knew that, it was hard to explain why it wasn't more of a draw to him. And when he looked up at Shelby, he knew he owed her a response.

"I'm very close to my mother and my sister," he began and then let out a soft laugh. "Well, with Mallory and I being twins you probably could guess that."

She nodded.

"My mom raised us." He paused. "My dad left when Mallory and I were five and we haven't seen or heard much from him since."

"Oh, my goodness! That's horrible!"

But Sam shook his head. "Not really. He wasn't overly interested in being a parent and having him around just created a really negative atmosphere. My mom used to try so hard to keep up appearances and I honestly think she was relieved when he finally left."

"Wow."

"Growing up, it was always the three of us. We're this tight little family unit and we did everything and went everywhere together." He paused. "It may sound crazy or maybe a little selfish, but...I don't know...I think I liked the idea of finally having my own identity. A place where I wasn't Susannah's son or Mallory's brother or Ezekiel's great-grandson. I was able to just be me – a guy who could walk around and live his life without they eyes of his family or the entire town watching him." He let out a mirthless laugh. "Lot of good that did me. Turns out the real me is just as much of a screw-up as the one linked to the family and it doesn't matter who's watching."

She was still wearing her sunglasses so he couldn't tell for sure what she was thinking, but when she stood up he had to admit he was more than a little confused. Stepping around the table, she came to stand beside him, her hand still in his.

"I don't think you're a screw-up," she said, her voice soft but firm. "I think you're an incredible man. A kind man." With her free hand, she caressed the side of his face. "You're someone I'm so thankful I met and who I love spending time with." She paused. "You don't give yourself enough credit. I like the man that you are, Sam."

God, she was sweet. Didn't she realize she was too good for him? Shouldn't it bother her more that he made so many mistakes or how so many people were disappointed in him? He studied her face long and hard as he struggled to find the right words to say. There was a small part of him that knew he should warn her – to tell her not to waste her time with him – but he couldn't because there was a much bigger part of him that needed her.

Needed her more than he had ever needed anyone in his entire life.

Shelby made him feel like he had a clean slate – she never talked about the things he did or the rumors she'd heard about him. In her eyes, it was like she met a stranger who she wanted to know. She didn't care where he came from or what he'd done before. She was simply interested in the man he was now.

She tugged on his hand until he stood up. She bowed

her head. "And what I'd really like is to spend some time with you...um...down below in the cabin."

Even though Sam heard the words, he was afraid to believe them. Reaching up, he cupped her chin. "Shelby?"

She looked up at him and Sam removed her sunglasses. He saw the uncertainty there right alongside the desire. She was such a contradiction at times and yet...he'd never wanted a woman more.

"Please," she whispered.

Then he nodded and let her lead the way to the tiny cabin below.

---

This was it.

This was happening.

This was her being a seductress.

As Shelby crawled onto the tiny bed she began to second-guess her plan. Maybe this wasn't the right place for them to make love for the first time.

There was nothing sexy about crawling in the small space, but when she turned around, the look on Sam's face said otherwise. He tugged his t-shirt up and over his head before tossing it to the floor. Next, he kicked off his shoes, but all Shelby could look at was his chest – tan and muscled and just a light dusting of hair...it was the sexiest thing she'd ever seen. He rested one knee on the bed and placed a hand on her calf and she felt herself shiver. Then he gently caressed her skin before sliding down beside her.

Everything about him felt wonderful – the warmth of his skin, the touch of his hand – and even as they lay there face to face doing nothing more than gazing at each other while his hand lazily touched her, it was enough to make her forget to be nervous.

The first kiss was tentative – a mere brushing of their lips – but after that, it was clear they both wanted more. Their tongues dueled as Shelby rolled onto her back and Sam carefully covered one side of her body. Her hand skimmed up his back and up into his hair to anchor him to her – not that she needed to. He seemed equally anxious to keep her as close as possible too.

She wished they had more room because she wanted to roll around with him, but part of her knew this confined space had its perks as well.

He breathed her name as his mouth moved across her cheek and down across her shoulder. With deft hands, he caressed his way down her body and swiftly removed her shorts. There was no shyness to her as she gladly kicked them away. Then Sam lifted up slightly and looked down at her.

"Damn, Shelby," he cupped her cheek in his hand. "You take my breath away." He paused again and gave her a lopsided grin. "When you took off your sweatshirt earlier, I thought I was going to have a heart attack." He played with the strap of her suit. "All this clingy fabric left little to the imagination and all I could think of was how I couldn't wait to see you out of it – to unwrap you like some sort of sexy present."

Blushing, she removed her hands from where they were resting on his shoulders and let them fall to the mattress. Her heart was beating so loud and so hard that she was certain she was going to pass out. How had she gone her entire life without a man looking at her like this? His gaze was so hot, so sexy, that it made her want to squirm and look away, but she couldn't. It held her captive.

"Sam?"

"Hmm?"

"Unwrap me. Please." She barely recognized the breathy voice, but it didn't matter. Sam's hands were already on the move and as he slowly peeled the Lycra from her body, she was too overwhelmed with sensations to utter another word.

His work-roughened hands felt incredible on her bare skin. She was overly sensitive everywhere right now and when she closed her eyes, it was as if he were touching her everywhere at once. Her legs were restless and she felt like she was on fire one minute and then chilled the next. The only thing she could think of was how she hoped she didn't freak out or embarrass herself.

Kissing his way down her body, Sam would stop and linger a little here, a little there – just enough to make her squirm – before moving on to another spot. Shelby felt worshipped by the time her bathing suit was on the floor, next to her shorts and his shirt. Turning toward him, she was just about to wrap one leg over his hip when she gasped and tried to sit up.

"Shelby? What's the matter? Are you okay?" he asked, panic and concern lacing his voice. No doubt he was having a flashback to the way she had reacted the same way the first time they kissed.

"I...I forgot something up on deck," she stammered nervously, one arm going over her breasts, covering herself.

*Great time to go shy, Shelby.*

He looked at her oddly even as he began to move off the bed. "Oh, okay," he said slowly, but he didn't look any less concerned. "What is it? I can go up and get it for you if you'd like."

*Ugh...kill me now*, she thought.

Averting her eyes out of sheer embarrassment, she said, "Um...yes. Please." She paused and quickly glanced at him and saw he was still watching her expectantly. "Condoms," she forced herself to say, her voice cracking slightly. "I...I put some condoms in the side pocket of the cooler bag and... and I forgot to bring them down here. So...yeah. Condoms."

*Oh, God. Can I say the word condoms any more?*

Sam instantly stopped moving and a slow smile played at his lips. "You brought condoms with you?" And yes, there was amusement in his voice.

Still unable to look directly at him, she focused on his shoulder as she nodded.

And then the greatest thing happened – standing up, Sam stripped down to his boxer briefs before he crawled back onto the bed with her so they were pressed together from head to toe. He rested his forehead against hers and gave her the sexiest smile she had ever seen.

They were skin-to-skin everywhere and it felt so good that her nerves and embarrassment seemed to simply go away.

*Thank God.*

"Shelby Abbott, were you planning on seducing me?" he asked in the lowest, gruffest tone she'd ever heard from him.

Licking her lips as his body settled over hers, she nodded.

"Tell me," he begged. "Because I think that is the sexiest thing ever."

"Really?"

He nodded.

She swallowed hard and hoped she didn't sound like an idiot. "I...I wanted to seduce you. I've been thinking about it for days." She looked away, embarrassed by what she was about to admit. "I've never done anything like this before. I went out and bought a different bathing suit – a bikini – but I wasn't brave enough to wear it. I thought it would look like I was trying too hard and I knew it would just distract me." Then she did look back at him. "But the other stuff...the... you know...I was hopeful and wanted to be prepared."

Tilting his head, he let out a breath next to her ear, giving her chills. "Can I let you in on a little secret?"

She nodded again.

"I was hopeful and prepared too," he whispered, licking the shell of her ear. "I'm glad we're on the same page." Then he gently bit the spot he had just licked and Shelby practically bucked off the bed.

"Really?" she asked again, knowing how ridiculous she was starting to sound.

"Yeah. Really." And then one finger traced along the side of her face, her jaw, down the slender column of her throat before stopping and teasing the swell of her breasts. "You're so beautiful, Shelby." He placed a light kiss on her shoulder. "So soft."

Her eyes fluttered closed as he rained soft, gentle kisses over all the places he had just touched. He wasn't doing anything to rush her, almost as if he was letting her set the pace. And as much as she was enjoying the slow seduction, she was ready for more.

"Sam?"

"Yes?"

"Are we going to put all that preparedness to good use?" And for the first time in her life, she embraced her boldness, maneuvering them until she was wrapping her arms and legs tightly around him.

Rocking gently against her, he replied, "Baby, we most certainly are."

The sun was going down and the air was definitely cooler as Shelby and Sam walked up to her house. She couldn't stop smiling and it seemed Sam was the same way. That made her feel even more tingly than she already did.

Sex.

*Wow.*

Yeah, it was hard to go beyond one syllable because he had completely blown her mind – multiple times. She had to fight the urge to giggle and blush just thinking about it.

After they had made love the first time, Shelby was fairly certain she had died and gone to heaven. It was a cliché, for sure, but it was exactly how she felt. She didn't know it was possible to be so thoroughly satisfied and invigorated even as she lay there exhausted and panting for breath.

Sam had gone up on deck to grab the remains of their lunch and dessert and they ate in the tiny bed. Part of her wanted to go up on deck and just...just...be naked in the sun and then make love again up there. Unfortunately, she wasn't *that* brave and when Sam had leaned in and licked a small spot of brownie icing from her lips, she had forgotten all about moving anywhere and simply reveled in the feeling of being loved by this man.

Best. Day. Ever.

She was slightly sunburnt from all the time they did spend out on deck and the plan was for them to come back to her place so she could shower and Sam would go pick up takeout for them for dinner.

And then hopefully spend the night.

Once inside the house, they worked together to unpack the few containers from the cooler bag and wash them – all the while finding excuses to be near each other. They kissed and laughed and talked about everything and nothing at all.

And it was amazing.

After a few minutes, Shelby took Sam by the hand and led him through the house and to her bedroom. It was the first time she was bringing him in here and she was glad she had waited because right now felt perfect. The bikini she had discarded earlier was on the floor and she caught Sam looking at it.

"Next time we go out on the boat, I promise to wear it," she said quietly, giving him a shy smile.

To her surprise, he walked over and scooped the two pieces off of the floor and let them dangle from his fingers. "Or...you could model it for me right now."

She could feel herself blushing.

From head to toe.

Put on the bikini now? Like...get changed right there in front of him? It seemed a bit scandalous and more than a little intimidating to her. "Uh...now?"

Laughing softly, he pulled her into his arms and kissed the top of her head. "Not if it makes you uncomfortable," he said. "But I have to admit, now that I've seen it, I'm going to be incredibly curious to see what you look like in it."

Before she could second-guess herself, Shelby grabbed the pieces and ran to the bathroom to change. Sure it seemed a little late for her to be playing modest after being naked with him for most of the afternoon, but...

"I'm a total chicken," she murmured, shutting the bathroom door behind her. She quickly stripped out of her one-piece and shorts and slipped on the bikini. Other than a quick glance in the mirror to finger-comb her hair, she refused to look at her full reflection so she couldn't chicken out of walking back into the bedroom.

With a steadying breath, she opened the door and found Sam lounging on her bed.

And he looked really good there.

He instantly sat straight up with wide eyes. "Damn, Shelby," he said in awe. "You look...incredible." Slowly, he came to his feet and walked over to her, which was good because she suddenly felt frozen to the spot. His warm hands settled on her waist as he hungrily looked her over from head to toe. "It's a good thing you didn't wear this earlier."

"How come?" she whispered.

His dark eyes met hers. "Because if you had, we might not have ever left the marina. I would have taken you down to the cabin and kept you there all day." He played with the bow on her hip and smiled. "Well this is certainly handy."

This time she did giggle. "You think so?"

"Oh, I know so." He gently tugged at the bow and his smile grew as it began to loosen.

And once that bow was loose, the other one quickly followed. Next thing Shelby knew, Sam was lifting her up. Her legs wrapped around his waist as he carried her over to the bed and they tumbled onto it.

They laughed even as they kissed, and as they rolled around on her queen-sized bed, she felt incredibly happy.

Plus, it was nice to experience making love with Sam in a real bed now.

The bikini top seemed to disappear under his deft hands and she did her best to help him undress just as quickly.

It was a little bit of a wonder for her that they were this ready to make love again. Ever since losing her virginity at nineteen, it had been her experience that you normally did it once, maybe twice, and then...that was it for the day.

Or the night.

But considering they had done it twice on the boat and they both seemed more than ready to go for a third time, she guessed she may have been misled all this time.

And she'd never been happier about being wrong about something!

It was amazing what being in a solid and sturdy structure could do, she thought. There was definitely something to be said about having four walls around you and a floor that wasn't rocking, even as the bed was.

When Sam rolled over onto his back and she sat up astride him, she felt empowered and by the way he looked at her, she felt beautiful.

Leaning forward, her hands cradled his face and she smiled. "Thank you," she said.

He quirked a dark brow at her before grinning. "Not that I'm complaining, but for what?"

"For this. For today. For...everything," she said sincerely. "I just want you to know this has been the best day for me and..."

She never got to finish because Sam reached up, fisted a hand into her hair and dragged her down for their steamiest kiss yet.

And then she was lost and it was well over an hour before she could even remember where she was or what day it was.

Her stomach growled loudly and she wanted to die of embarrassment.

Luckily, Sam's followed suit and they both ended up laughing.

"I think that's my cue to get up and go get us some dinner," he said, kissing her one more time before rolling off the bed. Sliding on his boxers, he looked down at her with a very satisfied look on his face. "Any chance you want to stay here like that so we can eat Chinese food naked in bed?"

She hummed as if considering it but then couldn't help but laugh. "Not a chance. I imagine there would be rice everywhere!"

"Oh, you're no fun," he teased as he finished dressing.

Shelby was up and doing the same – opting to put on a pair of yoga pants and a t-shirt rather than what she wore earlier. Honestly, she wished she could grab a quick shower while he was gone, but she wasn't sure she'd have enough time.

They walked out into the living room and Shelby called in their order. Hanging up, she looked over at him. "Ten minutes."

Sam chuckled. "It's always ten minutes, have you ever noticed that?"

At first she looked at him oddly, then realized he was right. "Oh, my goodness! I never did until now! That's wild!"

He was still grinning as he slipped his shoes on and gave her a quick kiss. "I'll be back in a few minutes." And then he was out the door.

Closing it behind him, she was about to make a run for the shower when her phone rang. She contemplated for all of three seconds before she walked over and answered it.

"Hey, Dad!" she said upon seeing his name on the screen. "How are you?"

"Hey, Shelly-bean! How's my girl today?"

As goofy as it was, the nickname always made her smile. Sitting down on the sofa, she put her feet up on the coffee table. "I'm good, thanks. What's up?"

"I was wondering if you could volunteer in the nursery

tomorrow? Mrs. Grant is down with the stomach flu. Can you cover for her?"

"Of course," she said happily. "You know I always love to have an excuse to go and snuggle babies! Who else will be in there with me?"

"Mrs. Mackie and Mrs. O'Hara," he said, "and Mrs. O'Hara's daughter, Elizabeth."

"Are you sure you'll even need me in there?" she asked. "It sounds like there's already more than enough hands on deck."

He laughed softly. "We have twelve babies under nine months old in there. Trust me – they need you."

"Okay, no worries. I'm your girl! I'll be there at eight. Will that work?"

"Absolutely. And thank you, Shelby. I appreciate you being willing to help."

"Nonsense, Dad. You know you only have to ask and I'm willing to help out. If I wasn't in the nursery, I'd probably be in one of the other children's ministry rooms."

"I wish you'd get to sit for a sermon once in a while."

"You and me both," she said with a small sigh. "But it's a good thing I can listen to it online."

"It was a great idea to make the sermons available online, Shelby. I can't thank you enough for that. So many of our parishioners have commented on how much they appreciate having the option when they're sick or away on vacation."

"I'd heard of other churches doing it and figured why not ours? Just because we're small doesn't mean we can't keep up with technology to help reach out to our church family."

"You make me proud, Shelly-bean."

"Dad..."

"Alright, alright, no teasing," he said lightly. "How about lunch tomorrow after church? Your mother is making a pot roast and we'd love to spend some time with you."

"That sounds great."

Maybe she could ask Sam if he'd like to join her...

Wait, was it too soon to introduce him to her parents?

"I've got some other calls to make to guarantee all the classes are covered tomorrow. Have a good night."

"Thanks, Dad! You too!" After she hung up, Shelby put the phone down and thought more about Sam and her parents. She'd never seen him at church before – and that wasn't necessarily a bad thing. Maybe he had a church back in Virginia that he went to and maybe he didn't want to get too involved in the community here since he didn't plan on staying. Or maybe no one had ever invited him to church before and she could be the one to do that!

That idea was a little exciting to her.

But...his mother attended and so did his sister and her fiancé...and his cousins.

Okay, so not ever being invited to church clearly wasn't the issue.

Getting to her feet, she decided to wait until he got back and simply ask him herself rather than sit and guess. To distract herself, she got out plates and silverware and placed them on the coffee table before heading back into the kitchen and pouring them each some sweet tea. She had wine on hand and some beer, but it had already been a long day and right now she wanted something a little more refreshing. If Sam wanted something different, he knew he could help himself.

When he walked in the door ten minutes later, she took the bag from him and placed it on the table just as she blurted, "Want to come to church with me tomorrow?"

He looked at her oddly for a moment. "Um...what?"

Shelby told him about the conversation with her father and how she would love for him to come to church with her and she'd find a way to get someone to cover the second hour of childcare so she could sit with him.

"Wait," he interrupted, "why are you volunteering in childcare? Doesn't the church have a staff for that?"

"We have volunteers," she explained. "And one of them is ill and my father called and asked if I could fill in." She smiled. "I'm sure if I called him back and told him I was bringing someone with me to church, he could find an additional volunteer to help out. What do you think?"

He was standing so still that Shelby almost wanted to reach out and touch him to make sure he was all right.

"Sam?"

Shaking his head slightly, he looked at her. His expression was a little bit pained. "Uh...who is your father?"

Smiling, she replied, "Steve Abbott. He's the pastor of Magnolia Baptist Church. Didn't you know that?"

7

Holy shit, Shelby's father was Pastor Steve? How had he not made the connection sooner? His stomach sank and everything in him told him to cut his losses and run. What was the point in sticking around when he knew it was only a matter of time before her father ratted him out and told her she could do better? It would hurt a lot less for him to end things now rather than have to deal with the reality of when she had to break up with him. No doubt she'd try to soften the blow, but all the while they'd both know why she was doing it.

And who was behind it.

And there was no way he could try to convince her she was wrong.

Slowly, he sat down on the sofa as it all sank in.

Although, Shelby already knew who he was when they first met and if her father had ever mentioned him or the things Sam had done, wouldn't she already know about them? Was it possible she was already aware of the many things he'd done that offended her father and she was choosing to ignore them?

Could he be that lucky?

"You okay?" Shelby asked, resting her hand on his knee. "You went a little pale."

It wasn't fair. Why today? If Sam had to pick one day in his life that was perfect, it would have been this one. For most of the day, it was like they had been in their own little world with nothing to worry about, no distractions, and no prying eyes. How was it that only an hour ago they were making love and now he had to give her up?

"Sam?"

Awkwardly, he cleared his throat. She had set up their dinner on the coffee table and was looking at him expectantly. There was no way he could just get up and walk out so he was going to have to suck it up and at least eat with her before coming up with an excuse to leave.

*But I really want to spend the night. If I have to give her up, can't I just finish out this perfect day by having her sleep in my arms all night?*

Of all the times in his life for his transgressions to come back and bite him in the ass, why did it have to be now?

When she said his name again, Sam forced himself out of his stupor and looked at her. "Uh...sorry. I sort of zoned out there."

She gave him a small smile. "Believe it or not, I'm used to it. I never should have asked about church."

Frowning, he asked, "What do you mean?"

With a sigh, she fussed with the containers of food. "The topic of church is personal and it makes a lot of people uncomfortable. I guess I should have eased into it before I just blurted it out. Sorry."

Reaching for her hand, Sam waited for her to look at him. "You don't have anything to apologize for," he said quietly. "The topic is...well...let's just say I'm a little more uncomfortable than most."

"How come?"

Ugh...why hadn't he thought it through before saying something like that?

A dozen thoughts raced through his head but none of them stuck. "Why don't we serve this up before it gets cold?" he said instead.

"I knew I shouldn't have brought it up," she murmured, grabbing a pint of fried rice.

"Can I ask you something?"

Nodding as she made up her plate, she said, "Sure."

"Are you close with your parents?"

She nodded again. "I am. I'm an only child and while I think that's probably a large part of it, I wouldn't say it's the only reason we're close. They're my rock – my biggest support group and my loudest cheerleaders. Even when they make me crazy," she said with a smile. "You're close with your mom, right?"

"I am," he said slowly. "But...like I was telling you earlier, a lot of that is because she had to be both mother and father to me and Mallory. We were a tight little unit because we were all we had. My grandparents passed away when Mal and I were young, and Pops and all our cousins lived here."

They ate in silence for a few minutes before Shelby asked, "How come you wanted to know?"

He shrugged. "Just curious."

And he was, but...he had no idea how to move forward from here. Breaking up would make things so much easier – for Shelby more than anything. If she was close to her parents, he didn't want to be the guy who got between them. Once he had dated a girl who neither his mother or Mallory liked. He had fought with the two of them more times than he could remember about it and, in the end, they were right.

Just like Pastor Steve and his wife would be about him.

Appetite gone, he placed his plate down on the table and sank back against the sofa, raking a hand through his hair. The timing would be awful, but considering his reputation, surely no one would be surprised.

But he had a feeling Shelby would – along with being incredibly hurt.

Beside him, she took another few small bites of food but he could tell she was concerned about his sudden change in mood. The last thing he wanted to do was ruin the night any more than he already had.

*Suck it up, buttercup. If this is your last night with her, you need to get your head out of your ass.*

"Want to watch a movie?" he asked, hoping he sounded a little more enthusiastic than he actually felt.

"Sure."

Yeah, he had definitely killed the mood. Now he needed to do something to bring it back.

Flipping on the TV, he pulled up Netflix and scrolled through some comedies in hopes that laughing would help him out. When she commented on some of her favorite comedians, Sam instantly found some stand-up specials and was relieved when they found one they both agreed on. Within minutes, they were both a lot more relaxed. He even reached out and picked up his plate to finish his dinner.

A little over an hour later, they were cleaning up their dinner mess and he caught Shelby yawning. Maybe he should go so she could get some sleep. He was about to suggest that when she walked over and wrapped her arms around him before kissing him.

"Mmm...what was that for?" he asked.

"For dinner. For a great day." She looked down and he saw the slight flush of her cheeks and found it so damn adorable that he hugged her tightly.

"It was all my pleasure. Trust me," he teased lightly.

She laughed quietly and then looked up at him again. "I was wondering if maybe...um...maybe you'd like to stay the night?"

"There's nothing I'd like more," he replied gruffly. He knew he was courting disaster, but there was no way he could say no to her. Not now.

Possibly, not ever.

---

"Wait...explain that to me again."

Sam rolled his eyes. "I've already explained it three times, Mason. What is your deal?"

It was Sunday afternoon and they were fishing off of Mason's boat. After leaving Shelby's that morning, he had texted his cousin with an SOS. There were so many things he needed to work out in his mind and a day on the water catching fish seemed like a great way to help put things into perspective.

Shrugging, Mason leaned back a bit and adjusted his line. "I can't help it if I'm confused. Everything you just said is messed up – like seriously messed up. You're really into this woman and she's really into you, but you're going to break up with her because it's going to be better for her in the long run. Do I have that right?"

"Uh...yeah." But somehow when Mason said it, it just sounded wrong.

"Cruel to be kind, is that what you're thinking?"

"Yeah."

Turning, Mason stared at him for several moments. "You're an idiot, Sam." Then he shook his head. "I cannot believe I used to think you were the coolest guy I knew."

"Hey!"

"That's what I'm thinking, hey!" Mason snapped.

"That doesn't even make sense!"

"And neither does what you're saying, dude! Come on! It seems to me you're not as into Shelby as you claim if you're so willing to just walk away."

Now he regretted being on a boat because all Sam wanted to do was storm off.

But he couldn't.

"You know, when you first mentioned how your mystery Shelby was Shelby Abbott, I thought you were crazy."

"Why?"

"Because I know who her father is. Plus, I went to school with her, Sam. We've both lived in this town our whole lives. She's a nice girl, but...you know...totally not your type."

"And what the hell is that supposed to mean?" he demanded.

"Exactly what it implies!" Mason retorted loudly with a huff of annoyance. "She's quiet, studious, a little mousy. She's not the type of girl you normally gravitate toward, so you'll have to excuse me if I find all of this a bit strange! What is it about this girl that has you so twisted up in knots? I don't get it!"

Okay, now he didn't want to storm off; he wanted to pound on his cousin.

Hard.

"When I look at her, I don't see all the ways that she's different," he explained, doing his best to remain calm. "All I see is this beautiful girl with a great smile, amazing eyes, who just makes me...I don't know...*feel*! She makes me laugh, she makes me think, but more than anything, she doesn't care about all the shit I've done. It's like I have a clean slate with her!" Pausing, he raked a hand through his hair. "I can't describe it, man, but from the minute I saw her it was like...crazy."

"You're crazy," Mason mumbled and then seemed to take a minute to collect his thoughts.

"You don't understand..."

"You're right," Mason agreed. "I don't." Then he snorted with disgust. "Because if this is how you really feel about her, do you realize how lucky you are?"

Sam rolled his eyes hard. "Right. I'm so lucky that the girl I'm dating is the daughter of the man who is probably my number one enemy in this town."

"Dude, he's a pastor. I'm pretty sure he doesn't consider anyone an enemy."

"You don't know that for sure."

"And neither do you! Dammit, Sam, you're ready to create a preemptive strike and there may not even be a reason for it! You need to at least test the waters first – see if he gives you an attitude or any kind of grief! For all you know, he'd just like to talk to you and maybe get an apology from you for drinking on church property, doing donuts in the church parking lot, and... you know...peeing on church property." The last one was said with a smirk and that just pissed Sam off more.

"Need I remind you how you were with me for all of those things?" he asked, his voice dripping with sarcasm.

"And yet I go to church most Sundays and never caught an attitude from the man. You should try it sometime."

Sighing loudly, Sam stared out at the water as he remembered Shelby's invitation to go with her to church. If Mason hadn't caught any grief, maybe there was hope for him.

Maybe.

But he couldn't be sure.

"I just don't think I could handle it if she were the one to break things off."

"Why?"

"Because she'd be doing it to appease her parents and we'd both know it. Then it's like...like confirmation that I didn't mean enough for her to fight for."

"First of all, conceited much?"

"Excuse me?"

"I mean, maybe she'd break up with you because you're a jackass or because she's just not into you. Have you ever thought of that?"

"Dude..."

"No, I'm being serious," Mason went on. "And you have to admit, you're not willing to fight for her either."

Damn. He hadn't really thought of it that way. In his mind, he was doing the right thing – the noble thing. He didn't see it as not being willing to fight for her, more like he was willing to make the sacrifice for her.

The old Sam would have been fine with dating her without giving a damn about what her parents or anyone thought about it. But for some reason, he had finally developed a conscience and he wasn't willing to be that guy anymore – he couldn't be.

"Do you have any idea what it's like to date someone your parents don't approve of?"

Mason let out a mirthless laugh. "Dude, you've met my parents. Hell, you're related to them. You know the only girls I ever bring home are ones they approve of because otherwise, I'd catch all kinds of hell from them. The only time I ever go out with a woman of my own choosing is when I'm out of town."

"You know that's a shitty way to live, right?"

"You're a fine one to pass judgment," Mason countered. "Let's just agree that we both aren't the poster boys for making good decisions and leave it at that."

They fished in companionable silence for several long minutes. It was peaceful and relaxing and yet Sam couldn't get his mind to shut down and enjoy it.

"So what if I don't exactly break things off with Shelby but we sort of...don't see each other every single day?"

"And what would be the point in that? Until you actually deal with her parents, nothing you do or don't do is going to prove anything. You're only going to make things worse on yourself by pulling back."

"Maybe."

"Let me ask you – have you slept with her yet?"

"None of your damn business," Sam snarled.

"So that's a yes," Mason said, grinning. "If you've slept with her and then suddenly pull away, you're going to look like a major douche, Sam. So if you're looking for excuses to help her break up with you, then yeah. Do that. But if you're serious about her and not wanting it to end, then man up and maybe meet her parents. Or at the very least, go and have a conversation with her father. He's looking for you to do some work for him, isn't he?"

"Not for him specifically, but on the church grounds."

"There's your opportunity. Go and meet with him and see what kind of reaction you get from him. If he's all judgmental and whatnot toward you, then you at least have something to base your decision with Shelby on."

Groaning, he threw his head back and let out a long breath. "The last thing I want to do is talk to this guy."

"I thought the last thing you wanted to do was lose Shelby."

Touché.

"I'm going to screw this up no matter what I do," Sam said after a moment. "It doesn't seem to matter what I do. I end up messing it up."

"You don't have to, Sam. Not this time."

If only...

"Every scenario I play out in my head ends badly. Even if her father treats me decently or is even neutral, I'm gonna be defensive and come off looking bad. If I break things off with her now, I'll look bad. If I stay and make things tense between Shelby and her parents, I'll feel bad." He looked over at his cousin. "You see? It's a no-win situation."

"And I still say you're wrong. You just need to get out of your own head."

"I don't even know how." Giving up on fishing for the time being, Sam pulled his line in and put the pole down. "It's this damn town!" he cried. "It just makes me crazy! If this sort of situation came up back home – back in Virginia – it wouldn't be like this! If I dated someone and her parents didn't like me, I could at least try to win them over. Or maybe I wouldn't even care because I wouldn't be as into the girl as I am with Shelby!" He growled in frustration. "It's not fair, dammit!"

Mason followed his lead, reeled in his line and put his

pole down. "When did you turn into such a damn drama queen?"

His only response was to give his cousin the finger.

"Okay, again...I think you're overreacting about the whole town thing. Personally, I don't think there's an angry mob just standing around waiting to point out your shortcomings or that there are tons of people here in town who are just waiting to be mean to you. I think that's all in your head."

Sam could only stare but he was fairly certain his jaw was on the floor.

As if reading his mind, his cousin grinned and nodded. "Doesn't Mrs. Henderson always give you free donuts when you go in there?"

"She does that for everyone."

Mason snorted with disbelief. "If she did that for everyone, she'd be out of business. And for the record, I've never gotten a free donut."

"Yeah, well..."

"And weren't you telling me that Mr. McHale at the nursery you use offered you some big discount because of all the business you're giving him?"

"Well that's just good business..."

"Didn't the town's festival committee ask you to join them in planning the Spring Fling Flower tour because you're – and I quote – 'the first person in thirty years who knows how to make things in this town bloom to showcase standards?'"

"I think you need a hobby if you can remember all the conversations people have had with me," he deadpanned.

Unfortunately, he wasn't deterred by Sam's snark. "What about the Winslows? The ones who own Beaches and Steam?"

Damn. He knew where this was going.

"Are we gonna fish or what?"

With a low laugh, Mason stared him down. "Do I need to remind you what the Winslows said to you when we stopped in there for lunch a few weeks ago?"

"Mason...come on, man. Let's just...you've made your point!"

"I believe it was Mr. Winslow who came over to the table and gushed at what a blessing you've been to the good folks of Magnolia Sound," he went on, his smile growing with each word. "He talked loudly enough for the entire dining room to hear about how your work with the cleanup and beautification after the storm makes everyone in town smile."

Sam rolled his eyes, but couldn't help but remember the sense of pride he'd felt at the compliment.

Stepping in closer, Mason's expression went a little somber. "The only one with a problem with you, is you. Now quit acting like a sniveling little bitch and man up!"

Sam wanted to be offended, but he knew it was exactly how he was behaving. Being a whiny man was not something he wanted to excel in, but right now he couldn't seem to stop himself.

"I don't know..."

With a huff of annoyance, Mason walked away, mumbling the entire time about Sam needing professional help. Pulling a bottle of water from the cooler they brought with them, Mason took a long drink before pointing the bottle at Sam. "You know what? If this is what falling in love does to a guy, I will gladly stay single, thank you very much."

His eyes went wide. "What? I never said I was in love with Shelby."

Grinning, Mason went and sat down on top of the cooler. "You didn't have to."

---

Six days.

It had been six days since she last saw Sam and it was slowly killing her.

Shelby had sworn to herself that she wasn't going to get too attached because she already knew Sam wasn't the kind of guy who did long-term relationships.

But she thought he'd last longer than a week.

Oh, he'd called her during the week. Twice. And both times he made sure she knew just how busy he was.

Yeah. Message received.

So why did it hurt so much?

And why had she told her parents she was dating someone?

"Ugh...I'm pathetic," she moaned as she walked out to her car on Friday after work. She had hoped to have plans this weekend – had hoped to perhaps introduce Sam to her parents – but clearly *that* wasn't going to happen. Off in the distance she heard the familiar sound of the lawn equipment, but when she looked over, Sam wasn't part of the crew.

No surprise there.

All the way home, she agonized over it. Why had he pulled away so soon? If he wasn't interested in things going any further, why not just talk to her? And really, what a jerk he was for doing this right after they had slept together! With every thought and every mile, her anger grew until she realized she wasn't even driving to her house, but to Laney's.

Pulling up to her driveway, she saw Laney stepping out the front door. Climbing from the car, she slammed the door shut. "We need to go out tonight," she declared and smiled at her friend's stunned reaction.

"Um...okay. But why? You didn't mention anything at work earlier."

Shelby explained everything she had been thinking while driving over. "So if this whole relationship is over, then fine. But I can't sit home and agonize over it or overanalyze it. Which we both know I'll do if left to my own devices." Throwing her head back, she let out a long breath. "Help me, Laney. Please."

"Like I'd ever say no," Laney teased, taking Shelby by the hand. Within an hour, they were both ready to go. "It's really early. Want to go grab some dinner first? Blue Fin Bistro has a great Happy Hour and the food there's great too."

Shelby agreed. "I've only eaten there a couple of times but it's always been good."

In agreement, they walked out to the driveway. "I'm going to drive," Laney announced.

"How come?"

"Because I think you're going to need an extra drink or two to get you out of your own head."

"But...what about you? Then you can't really drive."

"I don't need to drink. One night won't kill me. But if need be, we can call for an Uber when we're ready to leave and you can sleep here tonight."

She wasn't even going to argue. There wasn't a doubt in her mind that she needed a night out to help her not to think about Sam and what a jerk he was.

Or how attractive he was or how much she had enjoyed the sex with him.

The thought came to her mind with such force that she stopped and gasped.

"Shell? You okay?" Laney asked, turning and looking at her.

"What if this is all because I'm bad in bed?" Shelby cried in a hoarse whisper. "What if...what if *I'm* the reason Sam stopped calling?"

"Oh my God, you did *not* just say that!" Grabbing Shelby's hand, she dragged her over to the passenger side of the car. "Do not even think like that! Sam stopped calling because he's a self-centered jerk – end of story! And personally, I think it's great how he showed his true colors early so you know what kind of person you're dealing with."

"Maybe."

"No maybes about it! Now get in the car!" Once Laney walked around and climbed in on the driver's side, she picked right back up again. "Look, I get that it sucks and you're not someone who takes relationships lightly. For you to have slept with him, I know you had to have felt something pretty deep for him."

Silently, Shelby nodded.

They pulled out of the driveway and began heading toward downtown Magnolia. "And if Sam had paid any kind of attention to who you really were, he would know that, so...he's a self-centered jerk and bad things should happen to him."

Shelby couldn't help but smile. "You're a good friend, Laney."

"Screw that, I'm the *best* friend!" she said with a big grin. "Want me to go beat him up?"

Now she couldn't help but laugh. "Thanks, but...I don't think that would really help anything."

"You don't know that for sure," Laney argued. "I can be

fierce when I want to. And you know I've taken boot camp classes at the gym."

"And that's helpful...why?"

"Feel my arm!" Laney cried, holding her arm out and making a muscle. "I am in top shape! I'm not saying I can take someone as big as Sam Westbrook down, but I can certainly inflict a little pain."

Shaking her head, Shelby patted her friend's arm. "Maybe we can call that Plan B."

After that, Laney pretty much dominated the conversation so they wouldn't end up talking about Sam anymore. They arrived at the Blue Fin and opted for a table in the bar area. It was loud and a little bit crowded, but they were still able to maintain a decent conversation without yelling too much.

They ate sliders and, after Shelby had a glass of wine, she started to relax. This was definitely what she needed. As they ate, more people began to fill in the bar area and it got a little louder, but she was still feeling good.

After they finished their meal, Laney suggested they move from their table and mingle, but she wasn't ready yet. "Maybe after another glass," she said and was relieved when Laney agreed.

They talked about work and about some of the people they were seeing milling about and it was nice to sit back and people-watch for a little while. "See that guy over there?" Laney asked, leaning in close. "The one in the black t-shirt with the blonde hair?"

Shelby nodded.

"I think I want him to buy me a drink!"

Laughing, Shelby shook her head. "So your whole 'I don't need to drink' thing didn't last very long, did it?"

"Yeah, I know. I'm bad," Laney said, not sounding the

least bit apologetic. "But my plan is to maybe dance for a little bit, catch his eye and see what happens from there." Then she looked back over at Shelby. "We're going to dance, right?"

It wasn't her favorite thing to do, but it could be fun. "Sure. Why not?"

"That's the spirit!"

Laughing, Shelby got up and ordered another glass of wine but by the time she was back at the table, Laney was ready for them to hit the dance floor. Taking her glass with her, she did her best to drink and dance – not an easy feat considering she wasn't the most coordinated person, but she made it work.

One song led to another and another. They were joined by several friends and Shelby danced with a guy or two but she soon felt a little sweaty and more than ready for a break. Casually, she made her way across the floor and over to the bar where she ordered a bottle of water and drank half of it down almost instantly. It was nice to be able to catch her breath for a few minutes, but before she knew it, Laney was leading her back out onto the floor and Shelby soon found herself dancing with a guy who introduced himself at Ethan. She recognized him from around town – he worked at the bank – and he seemed like a nice guy. It didn't take long for her to start smiling and laughing with him and honestly, she was glad she had decided to come out tonight.

Until she turned around and saw Sam walking in the door.

Her heart began to pound like mad in her chest and Shelby instantly began looking around for an alternate exit so she wouldn't have to see him. Doing her best to appear casual, she began to maneuver herself and Ethan toward the corner of the dance floor. It was a little darker and she was sure he must have misread her intentions and she had to think fast to make sure she set him straight.

Leaning in closely, she spoke directly in his ear to be heard over the music. "I need to go! My ex just showed up and I'm really not in the mood to deal with him!"

Ethan nodded and replied, "Do you want to go someplace else?"

With him? No. Right now she just wanted to leave. Looking around she spotted Laney talking to the guy she had been eyeing earlier and felt really crappy about interrupting that.

*What to do, what to do?*

She glanced up at Ethan and saw him looking over her shoulder and there wasn't a doubt in Shelby's mind as to who he was looking at.

She could feel him behind her.

With a weary sigh, she turned around and faced Sam who – in turn – was glaring at Ethan.

*Oh, good grief.*

To his credit, Ethan stepped in close to her in a show of support. Only...it felt wrong and extremely uncomfortable. Unsure of what she was supposed to do or say, she stood there quietly and waited to see if one of them was going to say anything. After what felt like an incredibly long and awkward time, Sam finally looked down at her.

"What are you doing dancing with this guy?"

Seriously? *That* was his opening line?

Doing her best to hold in both her rage and disappointment, Shelby frowned as she said, "It's really none of your business." When she started to turn, he reached out and put his hand on her arm. This time when she looked at him, she knew she wasn't going to be able to hold anything back for much longer. "What do you want, Sam?"

"Can we talk?"

With a fake smile, she said, "Sure." And when Sam looked a little more relaxed, she added, "You can call me sometime next week. You know, when you're not so busy."

Yeah, it was satisfying to watch his expression fall.

Shelby – 1, Sam – 0.

He stepped in a little closer. "I was thinking something along the lines of now," he said firmly, his eyes never leaving hers.

With more bravado than she actually felt, she said, "Well that's too bad. You see I was thinking something along the lines of seeing you after you left my bed Sunday morning and yet..." She let him figure out the rest. Turning to Ethan, she was surprised to find that he was no longer there.

So much for him being a nice guy.

With an inward groan, Shelby wondered what she was supposed to do now. Without looking at Sam, she started to walk around him, but he stopped her again and this time, she definitely hit her limit. Moving away from him, she let out a huff of frustration. "What do you want, Sam?" she shouted, full of frustration.

And some of his confidence seemed to wither away – like he finally realized just how upset she was. He leaned in and said, "Can we please go outside and talk? Just for five minutes, Shelby. Please."

As much as she really didn't want to, she had a feeling it was the only way she was going to get rid of him.

"Fine." Without another word, she led the way across the bar and out the front door. She stepped out into the parking lot and kept going. There was a wide concrete path that divided the businesses from the beach access and she walked across it and still kept going until her feet hit the sand. It was foolish to keep walking, but for some reason, she felt like the sand and surf would help calm her a little. With a small shiver, she spun around to face him. "So? What do you want?"

And for the first time since she'd met him, Sam looked completely defeated. Shelby thought she'd feel victorious at making him feel as bad as he made her feel, but she didn't. If anything, now she felt even worse. She wasn't a mean or spiteful person and playing these kinds of games just wasn't in her. It was on the tip of her tongue to apologize, but he beat her to it.

"I'm sorry," he said quietly. He was standing several feet away and Shelby had to appreciate the fact that he wasn't any closer. Dressed in faded blue jeans and a navy polo shirt, he looked as good as he always did and even as annoyed as she was right now, she had to fight the urge to reach out and touch him. His sandy-colored hair blew in the wind and she had to fight to move her own hair out of her face.

"Why?" she asked after a minute. "Why did you do it? If you didn't want to see me anymore, all you had to do was tell me. It would have hurt, but I would have appreciated your honesty."

He didn't respond right away and Shelby couldn't help but keep talking. "It's okay, Sam. Really. I always knew we were too different to work out together. So if this is over, just say it. Please."

Still no response.

Now she was back to being annoyed. "Are we?" she asked, her voice shaking. "Are we over?" It was almost painful for her to ask the question. She felt weak and needy and more than a little embarrassed that she had to ask.

She expected more flimsy excuses.

She didn't expect such brutal honesty.

"I got scared," he said lowly, gruffly. "There...there are some things about me that you may or may not know and...I thought it would be better for you if I left you alone." He paused, his expression pained. "I'm sorry."

Well damn. How was she supposed to respond to that?

## 8

Sam had no intention of ever admitting such a thing to Shelby, but when he walked into the Blue Fin and saw her dancing with that guy, all rational thought had gone out the window. On top of that, he knew there was no way he could lie to her. She deserved to know the truth and he'd deal with the fallout from it no matter what.

Although, right now he was certain he'd never been so nervous in his entire life.

"You got scared?" she asked with a hint of sarcasm.

He nodded.

"And you thought it would be better to blow me off like I didn't even matter than to talk to me about it?" she yelled, and before he could respond, she was yelling again. "Do you have any idea how you made me feel? All week long I was beating myself up and thinking it was my fault – that I knew I wasn't enough for you! I was too boring and not pretty enough and that I was bad in bed! You made me hate myself, Sam!"

"Shelby, I..."

"No, you don't get to talk! You had all week to call and

talk to me!" She stomped her foot and her long hair blew wildly around her. She kept swatting at it and trying to keep it out of her face and the last thing he should do was laugh, but it was hard not to. "Now you're laughing at me? Seriously?"

"I'm not laughing at what you're saying, I swear!" he began in earnest. "But the wind is..." Then he turned them so her hair was blowing away from her face. "It was just awkward standing here watching you battle with the wind. Sorry."

He thought maybe his gesture would win him some points.

But he was wrong.

"I told you from the get-go that this wasn't going to work and you just wouldn't listen! You probably got a great big laugh out of stringing me along all week – pretending like you were interested – and how the mousy little town librarian was probably easier than any woman you've ever picked up in any bar! And then the icing on the cake was getting me to sleep with you! Well if that's the kind of man you are, you should know that you're disgusting! You are the worst human being I've ever met! Seriously...the worst!"

After another little foot stomp as she tried to come up with more insults, Sam knew he was going to have to do something to reel her back in. Once she realized how wrong she was about him and this entire situation, she was going to feel bad about hurling all these insults.

"I can't believe I let myself get swept up in the fantasy that you would even want a girl like me! If I could, I would erase the last month so I never would have met you! I never should have even talked to you in the bar that night! I should have ran the minute I saw it was you..."

Okay. He was done.

Hauling her in closely, he kissed her. It was hard and brutal and she put up a bit of a fight before melting against him. Sam's arms banded around her and he accepted her small punches and the kick in the shin.

Although...*ow!*

He had them coming. But when she calmed down and began kissing him back, he felt his first glimmer of hope.

His hand raked up and anchored into her hair to hold her to him as his tongue ruthlessly dueled with hers. She was just as frantic and wild and he was on the verge of throwing them both down onto the sand and having his way with her.

All week – all damn week – he had thought about her. She wasn't out of his thoughts for even one minute. He missed her, ached for her, and now that she was here, Sam knew he couldn't let her go again. To hell with the consequences. He would deal with all of them if it meant keeping Shelby in his arms, in his life.

He'd face her father and everyone in town if that's what it took because being without her was just too damn hard.

"Come home with me," he murmured against her lips, unwilling to break the contact.

She was breathless and panting. "What?"

He kissed her again. "Come home with me. Please."

With her hands cupping his face, she let out a small moan. "Dammit, Sam, don't do this to me again. Don't make a fool out of me."

When she went to release him and step back, he held her close. "I'm not. I won't," he vowed. "I swear to you. Come home with me and we can talk or we can sleep or... we can do anything you want, Shelby. Please."

Then he held his breath because he was certain she was

going to reject him and chalk up the last several minutes to madness.

She licked her lips as her eyes slowly met his. "We could go to my house," she suggested.

And as much as he knew they could – she lived closer and it was definitely more private – he wanted her to come home with him. The house wasn't his and he shared it with his mother, but there was something a bit primal in him right now that made him feel strongly about taking her home to his bed.

And that's what he told her because he wanted to be completely honest with her.

"Tonight, I want you in my bed," he said, raining kisses along her cheek, her lips, her jaw. "I want to hold you in my arms all night and know that you're home with me."

"Sam..."

"If you want me to take you home at any time, I will, Shelby. Whatever it is you want, we'll do."

Her shoulders sagged slightly. "Please don't make me regret this."

And he hated that she even had to say those words out loud. He'd done that to her – made her doubt herself – and he knew he would do whatever it took to make it up to her.

Wordlessly, he took her by the hand and started to walk toward the parking lot, but she stopped him. "I need to text Laney and let her know what's going on," she said. "I came here with her."

He nodded and waited for her to do what she had to do, and once she was done and slid her phone back into her purse, he took her hand again as they walked over to his truck. "I should probably do the same with Mason. I met him here, but still." Pulling out his phone, he shot off a quick text and then turned it off. He didn't want any more interruptions.

And no doubt his cousin was going to blow up his messages with a bunch of "I told you so" texts.

Sam helped her into his truck and hated having to let go of her hand even for the minute it took him to walk around and climb in on the driver's side. As soon as he was situated, he immediately reached for her again. They drove in silence and as he pulled up to the massive family home which still resembled a construction zone far too much for his liking, he began to second-guess his decision to bring her here. It was a mess and he wished more than anything that he was taking her somewhere special and private. A place that was just for them. But it was too late now. They were here and he didn't want to spend any more time sitting here in his truck.

Within minutes they were in the house and after offering her something to drink, they walked up the back stairs to his room. Luckily in the last week, he had managed to help the work crew clean up a bit and he didn't have nearly as much debris in what he referred to as his "wing" as there had been. In his room, he turned on the light and closed the door behind him – watching as Shelby took in the space. When he saw her giggle, he had to ask, "What's so funny?"

Looking over her shoulder at him, she said, "I just had the feeling like I was back in school and sneaking into a boy's house."

Suddenly he wanted to punch any boy she might have done that with.

"Did you ever do that?" he asked. "You know...sneak into a guy's house after his parents were in bed?"

She laughed again. "Oh, my goodness, no. No boy ever

asked me to do something like that." She shook her head. "Don't be ridiculous." Then she shrugged. "But I always imagined what it would be like."

Relief washed over him.

Shelby primly sat down on the edge of his bed and looked up at him expectantly. They needed to talk – he knew that – but he needed to be with her more right now.

Slowly, he walked over and sat down beside her. One hand reached out and caressed her cheek, combing her hair behind her ear. "Thank you for being here."

Her smile was slow and sweet and just a little shy. "I don't know what I'm supposed to do, Sam," she said, her voice so low it was almost a whisper. "I know what I want to do, but I'm not sure it's the right thing. I don't like second-guessing myself and I certainly don't want to make a fool out of myself either."

He nodded because he knew exactly how she felt. "Yeah. Me too." Moving closer, he rested his forehead against hers. "I know we have a lot to talk about – and we will, I promise – but I missed you so much this week. More than I thought possible." There was hurt and disappointment written all over her face and it just about killed him all over again.

"I really wish you would have been honest with me," she said after sitting quietly for several minutes. "There are going to be things that aren't comfortable to talk about. We're going to disagree at times, but it doesn't mean you just shut down or...or lie because you don't want to have those discussions."

"I know. I realize that now. This is all new to me, Shelby."

"How is that possible? You're a grown man, Sam. You can't tell me you've never had an honest conversation with anyone. And I'm not even talking about girlfriends, just...anyone."

Now he knew she was going to be disappointed in him because unfortunately, that pretty much did describe him. "I tend to avoid awkward situations," he admitted lowly. "It's one of the reasons I'm even here in Magnolia. My great-grandfather knew that about me and this was his way of forcing me to stay in one place and deal with all my shit." Putting some space between them, he let out a long breath. "The only person I can honestly say I've ever had honest conversations with, is Mallory. But it's a twin thing. I couldn't keep anything from her even if I tried."

"I guess that's something," she murmured.

"You need to know that I'm trying. I'm really trying to change, Shelby."

"I'm not asking you to," she said sadly. "I don't look at you and think of all the ways you need to change. I started seeing you because I like you – genuinely like you as a person. Please don't think you have to make all kind of changes and sacrifices in order to be with me, Sam."

"You might not be saying that if you knew..."

She placed a finger over his lips before he could finish. "No. We're not playing that game, okay? I didn't come here so you can have some sort of confessional time. That's not what I need from you."

And as much as he wanted to argue with her, he didn't. He couldn't. If he didn't kiss her again soon, he just might lose his mind. "What is it you do need from me?"

Her smile was back as she inched her way closer. "I need for us to stop talking for a little while."

Now it was his turn to smile. "Only for a little while?"

"Well...maybe for a long while. Maybe all night."

He leaned in and inhaled her perfume before kissing

her shoulder and then her neck. "What about dirty talk? Does that count?"

She purred as his mouth moved over her skin. "I think dirty talk is totally fine," she said breathlessly. "Actually, the more the better."

*This girl*, he thought. How could someone who looked so sweet be hiding such a sexy side?

Doing his best to move things along, he maneuvered them onto the bed so he was stretched out beside her. Then he did his best to strip her down to nothing but her panties – which were white lace with little pink bows.

"Damn, Shelby," he said, his hands moving over her as he stretched out on top of her. "Had I known you were wearing these I would have stripped you down sooner."

When he looked up at her face, she was biting her bottom lip and smiling at him. "I hope it was worth the wait."

And then he was done taking things slowly. There would be time for that later. "You're more than worth it. But now I'm going to apologize one more time."

She looked up at him curiously. "For what?"

Completely covering her body with his, he kissed her deeply before responding. "Because I'm about to make up for a week's worth of missing you – hard and fast."

Her legs slowly came up and wrapped around him and then her arms. "Oh my..."

"Brace yourself," he said gruffly.

"Right back at ya," she replied.

And much later, it would be hard for him to say just who blew whose mind.

The room was fairly bright with sunlight, but Shelby didn't mind. Sam was wrapped completely around her and she was loving every minute of it. Of course, she would have loved a few more hours of sleep too, but it was worth the sacrifice to have spent the night being so thoroughly loved.

"Are you hungry?" he asked, his voice soft and sleepy.

She shook her head and snuggled closer. Their legs tangled together and she couldn't help but smile when she felt him kiss the top of her head. "I have no idea what time it is but I don't want to leave the bed yet."

His low chuckle sounded sexier than it should have. "I could go downstairs and make you something and bring it back up here if you'd like."

Shelby lifted her head and looked at him as if he were crazy. "You don't have to do that."

His expression was somber, serious. "But I would," he said, his hand reaching up to caress her cheek.

As his dark eyes scanned her face, Shelby read so many emotions there. And as much as she didn't want to do anything that could break this spell and take them from this warm and cozy cocoon they had made for themselves, there were things they needed to discuss.

Especially if this relationship was going to last beyond breakfast.

Swallowing her fears, Shelby met his gaze and voiced her concerns. "I don't want to leave here and know this was it – like this was just one last...hoorah." She almost groaned at her choice of words. "If that's all we have – if this is a relationship that is only going to work while we're naked and in bed – then I'd rather know that now, Sam."

There was such an overwhelming sense of sadness radiating off of him and Shelby wished she could take the words back. If she was wrong – if she had completely misread the situation and had, indeed, offended him – she wouldn't be able to live with herself.

His eyes no longer held hers and if anything, she thought he needed it to be that way. "I didn't know you were Steve Abbott's daughter," he began after letting out a long breath.

"O-kay…"

"I have a bit of a…history with your father," he went on. "And not a good one."

Shelby pulled back and looked at him, waiting for him to explain further.

When he ran down the list of all the things he'd done that involved the church and church property, she wasn't sure if she should laugh or cry.

"And that last one wasn't that long ago, so…"

"Oh, my gosh! *You're* the guys in the parking lot?" she cried and then began to laugh.

Hysterically.

Until she almost couldn't breathe.

Beside her, Sam sat up and did not look the least bit amused. "This isn't funny, Shelby!"

Clutching the sheet to her, she sat up and did her best to stop laughing. It took several attempts but when she finally did, she wiped the tears from her eyes and cleared her throat. "Okay, first of all, yes, it is funny."

"Shelby…"

Holding up a hand to stop him, she nodded. "Uh-huh. It is. Hysterical, actually. Is that why you stayed away last week? Because of who my father is?"

"Well…"

"Because that is the craziest thing I've ever heard! My father is the least judgmental person I know! And I'm not saying that because he's my dad, but because it's the truth!"

"I don't think you realize…"

"Sam, growing up, my father shared a lot about the things he saw and the people he met. He wasn't betraying a confidence or anything, but he's a people-watcher by nature. We've had people come through the church who have done things far worse than anything you've done and you know what? My father always welcomed them with open arms. It's not his place to judge. It's his place to lead by example and to teach forgiveness. If you had a conversation with him…"

"Yeah, uh…I've been kind of avoiding that. Hard," he added for emphasis.

It was all starting to make sense. This was a pattern of behavior for him – avoidance. And that simply wasn't going to work for her.

"Do you want to be with me?" she asked, her voice firm and commanding. "And I'm not just talking about here in bed, but do you want a relationship with me outside of this? Do you want to go on dates and hang out and…and…I don't know…just be together?"

"You know I do, Shelby."

"Do I? Because it seems to me like you'd rather run and hide than have what might be an awkward conversation! Or it could be great! Here's the thing, Sam, you don't know! No one is going to know until you actually try!" Tossing the blankets aside, she jumped off the bed and began to get dressed. She'd managed to pull on her panties and nothing more when Sam grabbed her arm and pulled her back onto the bed, pinning her beneath him.

"Believe it or not, I wasn't avoiding it because I was being a coward, but I was avoiding it because I didn't want to make any problems between you and your father," he snapped, but there was very little heat behind his words. "I can be a pretty confrontational guy if the situation calls for it, but this one seemed more like an 'I should step aside for Shelby's sake' sort of thing." He growled with frustration. "But no matter what I do or did, it seems like it's a no-win situation. Either we're both miserable because we're apart, or you're fighting with your father because he doesn't approve of me, or...or..."

"Sam, my father isn't going to approve of you not matter what," she stated simply and almost laughed at the shocked expression on his face. "I'm his only daughter and there hasn't been one guy I've dated that he's approved of – and that's including the ones he fixed me up with!"

He pulled back, straddling her. "Your father fixed you up on dates? That's just...weird."

Rolling her eyes, she pushed him off of her before resuming the task of getting dressed. "It's not that weird. He'd meet a new youth pastor or a seminary student and – in theory – would think they'd be perfect for me...but he was way more critical of them than I ever was. I just wasn't interested because there was no spark. My father, however, would find all kinds of crazy things to nitpick over. So you need to know going in, his not liking you for me will have nothing to do with you messing around on church property and everything to do with no one being good enough for his little girl."

"But it certainly isn't going to help," he murmured.

Once she was fully dressed, she turned and faced him. "What is it you want me to do, Sam? What can I possibly say to make you feel better?"

In a move she wasn't expecting, he reached out and pulled her back onto the bed where he kissed her as thoroughly as he had done everything else over the last ten hours. Shelby totally let herself get lost in the moment and it was easily another thirty minutes before they were heading down to the kitchen to get some coffee.

Where they came face to face with Susannah and Colton.

Sam stopped so suddenly that Shelby walked right into him. "Sam? Are you...?" Then she saw the older couple and couldn't help but gasp. Susanna was wearing an oversized t-shirt and nothing else and Colton had on a pair of jeans that were open and nothing else. "Um..."

"Sam! I didn't realize you were home," Susannah said, slipping behind Colton who looked beyond uncomfortable. Then she gave them both a weak smile. "Hey, Shelby. It's nice to see you."

Blushing, Shelby forced herself to smile. "Nice to see you too, Ms. Coleman."

"You just saw my mom without her pants, Shell," Sam said with a mild embarrassment. "I think you can call her Susannah."

"There's no need to be disrespectful," Colton said, taking a step toward Sam.

"You might want to zip up, Colt, before you finish that thought," Sam replied mildly as he walked across the kitchen. Looking at Shelby over his shoulder, he asked, "Want some coffee?"

What she wanted was to pretend she wasn't seeing what she was seeing, but that wasn't going to happen, so...

"Uh, sure. Thanks." She slowly made her way over to the kitchen table and sat down, looking out the huge back window at the Sound rather than at the people around her.

"Excuse me," Susannah murmured as she walked out of the room – no doubt to get dressed. In the distance, Shelby heard the sound of a zipper and figured that was Colton's contribution, but she still didn't feel confident in turning around.

Sam placed a mug in front of her as he sat down beside her. He stared down into his own mug and she knew she had to say something. "You okay?"

He lifted his head and gave her a small smile. "Sure. Why wouldn't I be? Nothing like an awkward encounter in the kitchen with my mom and her boyfriend who obviously just had sex," he murmured lowly.

Leaning in closely, she whispered, "They might feel the same way – only they'd be thinking how it was us who just had sex. And we'd all be right."

Groaning, he lifted his mug and took a sip. "Not helping."

Unable to help herself, she laughed softly. "Neither is sitting here pouting, Sam. It happened, it was awkward, and everyone's going to move on, end of story. It's not like we walked in on them doing it."

"You don't understand."

After taking a sip of her own coffee, she couldn't help but point out the obvious. "And this wouldn't have happened if we just went to my place last night."

Glaring at her, she could see all the annoyance and frustration. It was pointless to mention how if he had his own place this also wouldn't have happened, but that would just start another awkward conversation.

"Okay," Susannah said as she breezed back into the room. "Colton and I were going to make pancakes. Would the two of you like some?"

"You don't have to make us breakfast, Mom," Sam said, even though he was looking at the mug in his hand rather than his mother.

Shelby looked up and caught the sad look on Susannah's face and, as much as she wished they weren't currently sitting here together awkwardly, she also knew there was only one way to make things better.

"Actually, I would love some," Shelby said brightly. "Thank you!" Standing, she walked over to them. "Can I help with anything?"

And just like that all the tension seemed to leave both Susannah and Colton. The three of them talked casually about the house and the renovations and the overall plans for the bed and breakfast while Sam continued to sit and drink his coffee. Several times, Shelby caught Susannah glancing over at him and wished he would just stop being ridiculous and join them. By the time they were putting batter on the griddle, she'd had enough.

Walking over to Sam, she gave him a slight smack on the back of the head.

"Ow!" he said, looking up at her. "What was that for?"

"You need to get up and join the conversation," she said with a little snap to her voice. "We're all adults here, so...try acting like one." When she went to turn away, Sam reached for her hand and stopped her.

"You're kind of bossy this morning," he said, but his lips were twitching.

"I'm kind of bossy all the time, but you just haven't seen it yet."

Chuckling, he hauled her in close as his smile grew. "No, you're not, but that's okay. You're perfect the way you are."

She wasn't sure if she should be annoyed by how he called her bluff or happy for complimenting her. Kissing him on the cheek, she opted to think he was sweet. "I could be bossy if I wanted to."

Standing, Sam hugged her close. "I'll consider myself warned."

They joined Susannah and Colton and worked to finish getting breakfast together and by the time they all sat down at the table, Shelby was certain the awkwardness was over.

"So what are the two of you up to today?" Susannah asked.

Shelby looked over at Sam and shrugged because they hadn't really discussed anything. "I need to get some work done around the house," she said. "Laundry and then mowing the lawn."

"You mow your own grass?" Sam asked, and when she nodded he asked, "Why?"

With another shrug, she cut into her pancakes and picked up a forkful. "Why not?" she countered. "It's a small yard and it seems pointless to pay someone to do it. Besides, I don't mind."

It wasn't a total lie. In all honesty, there had been plenty of times she contemplated hiring a landscaper to take care of it for her, but it seemed like a poor decision to make when she did her best to be frugal. It was a form of exercise and forced her to be outside for a little while.

Usually cursing the entire time.

"I can help you with it today," Sam said. "That is, if you'd like me to."

*Don't appear too anxious...*

"Uh..." All eyes were on her. "Sure. That would be great. Thanks!"

They all ate in companionable silence for a few minutes before Susannah spoke again. "Sam, were you able to order the new shrubs for the backyard path that we talked about? Colton was saying how all of the construction debris and equipment will be out of the yard this week and I'd love to start cleaning it all up."

Nodding, he replied, "Everything's ordered and some of it's already at the nursery waiting for us to get started. Have you given any thought to what you want to do around the sides of the house? Are we sticking to what's already there or do you want to add something new?"

Then he launched into descriptions of various plants that left Shelby feeling more than a little impressed. It was obvious Sam was extremely knowledgeable about his career and considering it wasn't something he went to school for, she found herself to be a little in awe of him.

Rather than contribute anything or even ask any questions, Shelby was content to sit back and enjoy her breakfast while listening to him talk. It gave her some insight into him she wouldn't normally have. For all of his talk about not wanting to be here in Magnolia, there was definitely a passion in him for what he was doing that he wouldn't have when he went back to Virginia. It seemed like back home, he worked more random jobs rather than something he really enjoyed. Maybe she'd mention it to him at some point, but not today. Not when he was smiling and looking relaxed and sounding so happy as he shared his ideas for the property.

"Any chance you have some time to help me move some furniture?" Colton asked when the topic of landscaping was over.

"What furniture?"

"We're ready to start working on what used to be Mallory's room," Susannah chimed in. "We're going to move the furniture down into the cellar for now. I thought it would be best if we started emptying the upstairs room to make it easier on the crew."

Sam's room was upstairs, Shelby thought, and wondered how it must be for him living in a construction zone.

"Sure," Sam said easily, finishing his last bite of pancakes. "That shouldn't take too long." He looked over at Shelby. "I can take you home first, if you'd like, and then come over after lunch to take care of the lawn."

It was on the tip of her tongue to offer to help, but she really wasn't dressed for it. She was still wearing her skinny jeans and blouse from last night. Then she suggested, "How about you take me home so I can change and then I'll come back here and help?"

His eyes went wide. "Really? You want to help move furniture?"

"Oh, Shelby, sweetie," Susannah said, reaching across the table and patting her hand. "You don't have to do that. I couldn't ask you to."

"I really don't mind," she said. "I can toss in the first load of laundry when I go in to change and we can be back here in thirty minutes tops. I'm not sure I'll be able to lift any of the heavy stuff, but I can certainly help with smaller things or even cleaning up behind them."

"Well, it's all getting worked on so no need to clean, but I certainly won't say no to an extra pair of hands!"

"Great! Let's make a day of it!"

## 9

EVERYTHING WAS different and for the life of him, Sam had no idea how it happened. After that breakfast, his whole world seemed to change. It wasn't necessarily a bad thing, but...as he stood in Shelby's laundry room folding his clothes, he had to wonder just how he had gotten here. One minute he was moving furniture, the next he was moving out.

Well...sort of.

Stepping out into the living room, he looked around. Shelby was at a book club meeting and he was here in her house alone...why?

"I'm seriously losing it," he murmured, then walked to the kitchen where he'd left his phone and called Mason.

"Hey! You're alive!" Mason joked. "Did the wife say it was okay for you to call?"

"Ha, ha. You're hysterical," Sam replied. "What are you doing tonight?"

"I have a date."

"Nice! Anyone I know?"

An angry groan was his cousin's first response. "I wish it wasn't anyone *I* know."

"What does that mean?"

"My folks set me up to go out with Jessica Perkins. Her father is a lawyer here in town and her brother is a congressman. They thought we'd make a good match."

Sam had to stifle a laugh. "And why is that?"

"Because they have officially begun their campaign to convince me to go into politics. They figure if I start hanging out with political families it will wear off on me."

"Good lord..."

"Yeah. Tell me about it."

"And what's Jessica like?"

"Blonde, blue eyes, decent body..."

"Okay, not what I was talking about. What is she like? What does she do for a living? Do you have anything in common with her?"

Silence.

"Uh...Mason?"

"What's happened to you?"

"What do you mean?"

"I mean every time we've ever discussed women – ever – the only thing you ever cared about was what they looked like. What difference does it make what her interests are?"

Sitting on the sofa, Sam raked a hand through his hair and was about to argue how his cousin was wrong but...he couldn't. That really had been the only thing he ever thought about before but since he met Shelby, it just seemed wrong to judge a person on that. Hadn't they both been stereotyped that way? And once he saw beyond her librarian look – which was seriously way hotter than he ever thought possible – and got to know the woman she was, he realized how superficial he'd been his entire life.

"I don't know. I just figured I'd ask, that's all."

"Liar. But I'll let it slide," Mason said wearily. "Jessica works in PR and is on the board of several different local charities. Her hobbies include horticulture, horseback riding, and long walks in the park."

This time Sam did laugh. "Please tell me you're reading her social media bio or something."

"Yeah, I wish. That's the text I got from my mother when I asked what she was like." He groaned again. "Seriously, I have zero in common with her. She graduated with my sister so she's younger..."

"Which sister?"

"Peyton. So she's only three years younger but..."

"Does Peyton know her?"

"Yeah."

"And?"

"In a way that only my sister has with words, she said – and I quote – 'Homecoming queen slash prom queen slash mean girl nightmare all rolled up into one.' End quote."

"Yikes."

"Yeah."

"And you agreed to go out with her why?"

"Like I had a choice. I would have been nagged to death until I did and if by some chance I still held out, this chick would have started showing up at family events or even just Sunday dinner. Trust me. I know how my mom works."

"Dude, you have seriously got to put your foot down. This is getting crazy. You're an adult. Act like one!"

"I don't know...maybe she won't be that bad..."

And that was it. For some reason, Sam felt it was time to say the words out loud that he swore he'd never admit to Mason.

"Look, when we were growing up, I hated you."

"Okay, that was hurtful."

Rolling his eyes, he continued. "No, I'm serious, Mason. And honestly, I don't even think it had a whole lot to do with you, personally, but the way your parents always talked about you. They boasted and bragged about every little thing you did and to tell you the truth, most of it wasn't all that impressive!"

"Hey!"

"Then as we got older, I watched you transform from this skinny, dorky kid into a kind of cool guy."

"Thanks, I guess..."

"And then you surprised me even more by bulking up and turning into a guy I not only consider a good friend, but one I think could kick my ass if I provoked him enough."

"You're well on your way to that right now..."

"The point is, they have been putting you in this box your whole damn life and you've let them! If you don't want to go out with this girl, then don't! And if they give you any shit about it, it's okay to fight back! What's the worst they can do?"

"They can make my life miserable..."

"They're already doing that! What more can they possibly do that they're not already doing?"

"Dude, you don't get it. I'm still living with them. I know it was supposed to be temporary, but..."

"Oh, my God. You need to move out!"

"Really? Ya think? Like I haven't thought of that already?!" Mason snapped sarcastically.

"Okay, first, relax."

"Sam..."

"No, hear me out. You need to move out so they're not going to know what you're doing and who you're doing it with – no pun intended." But he laughed anyway. "It's time! You know the only reason you moved back in with them was because it was going to be temporary."

"And yet, here I am. Still."

"Only because it's comfortable and easy. Hell, that's why I'm living with my mother."

"Are you?" Mason asked. "Because last I checked you were moving a bunch of your crap into Shelby's."

"That's only because of the construction. It's not like we're *really* living together."

"Yet."

"Dude, come on."

"Sam, Pops' place is huge. There are like eight bedrooms in there and they're all not currently under construction. If it was time for your room to get work done, there were plenty other rooms in the house for you to use temporarily. Admit it. You opted to move in with Shelby and you're not leaving anytime soon."

"Yeah, no. That's not what's happening. That would imply that I'm planning on staying in Magnolia, which we both know I'm not. That's not part of the plan." And even as he said it, the words sounded wrong.

"Then what are you doing, Sam? Why are you leading this girl on?"

"I'm not!" he denied.

"Aren't you? A girl like Shelby? For all intents and purposes, you're living with her – the pastor's daughter might I add – and you don't think you're sending out mixed signals? You don't think she's going to be devastated when you decide to high-tail it back to Virginia when your year is up?"

"I haven't...I mean, we never..."

"Are you suddenly thinking about not going back when your year is up?"

"I didn't say that, but..."

"But what? Are you even taking Shelby's feelings into consideration on this? Do you expect her to do the long-distance thing or are you just passing the time right now?"

"We're definitely not passing the time," he said with frustration, "but at the same time, I don't know what all this is! I've never done this before...never felt this way before! I didn't plan for this and I have no idea how to plan for the future, so...shit."

"Yup. Shit."

Now it was Sam's turn to groan. "The last thing I want to do is hurt Shelby."

"Yeah, we've had this conversation before – not that long ago either. And yet...man, you really suck at this. What she sees in you, I'll never know."

It was on the tip of Sam's tongue to make a crude remark, but...that didn't feel right. Not where Shelby was concerned.

"Weren't we talking about you and how you need to get a place of your own?" Sam asked with a hint of sarcasm.

"Unfortunately, yes," Mason agreed. "But it still doesn't get me out of this date tonight."

"You can always cancel."

"I'm not going to do that."

"Why?"

"For starters? It's rude. I may not want to do this, and I know I'm going under protest, but to cancel now wouldn't be right and I'd end up getting pressured into rescheduling."

Shaking his head, Sam had to wonder if his cousin real-ized how wrong his logic was. "Dude, if you go and you're not into it, you're going to come off as being rude too. It's a no-win."

"Yeah, but at least with my way I'm going out for a nice dinner and possibly getting laid."

Hard to argue with that.

"And you don't think sleeping with her and not going out with her again is a smart move?"

"Who is this?" Mason said with a mirthless laugh. "Because the cousin I know would be all for getting laid and never going out again. What's going on with you?"

Rubbing a hand over his face, Sam let out a long breath. "I think I'm developing a conscience."

"Well, damn. It's about time."

"Shut up. Now you need to get one."

"I will. Tomorrow."

They both laughed. "Look, you know what's best for you and I'm only looking out for you. I'm afraid your folks are going to keep pushing you until you end up married to someone you can't stand just because they're from the right family. You're a great guy, Mason, and you deserve to be happy. And that includes working in the field you want and dating the women you choose. Remember that."

"Thanks, man. I appreciate it. And just so you know, I get it. I know I'm as much to blame as they are in all this – probably more so – and I'm working on it."

Somehow Sam doubted it, but now wasn't the time to bring it up. "If there's anything I can do to help..."

"I know and it means a lot to me." He paused. "And something else you should know – it would really be great if...you know...you didn't leave when the year was up. I think if you chose to stay here in Magnolia, it would be good for you. For all of us. I like having you around." He let out another low laugh. "Believe it or not, you're like...you're more than my cousin, man. You're like a brother to me and it's been nice hanging out with you the last few months."

Damn. Sam felt himself getting choked up. This was the most meaningful conversation they'd ever had.

Ever.

And since they were...

"Well, you should know I feel the same about you. I never thought it would be that way – you know, since I hated you when we were growing up..."

"Um...ow..."

"But yeah...you've made being here a lot more...tolerable than I thought it would be. So...thanks."

"I feel like we should hug this out," Mason said, and Sam could tell he was only partly kidding.

"Dude, don't make me come over there," Sam said, laughing.

"Okay, fine. Ghost hug. Happy?"

That just made him laugh a little harder. "I feel like I should go back to not liking you just for saying ghost hug. Who are we, twelve-year-old girls?"

"Way to ruin the moment. Geez," Mason snorted. "But...I need to go. I'm supposed to pick up Jennifer..."

"Jessica."

"Right, Jessica. I'm supposed to pick up Jessica in about thirty minutes and I need to finish getting ready. What are you doing tomorrow? Wanna go fishing?"

"God yes! I'll meet you at the dock at seven."

"Sounds like a plan."

When Sam hung up and put the phone down, he felt... happy. Genuinely happy. He thought about their conversation and while Mason had largely played a part in making Sam's stay here in Magnolia tolerable, he wasn't the only reason. Once he got over being bitter about being forced to live here, he realized he had a lot here in Magnolia – his mother, his sister, his cousins, and, of course, Shelby.

He had no idea where this was going or how to even be in a long-term relationship. As it was, this was the longest relationship he'd ever been in. The only thing he could say for sure was that he wasn't ready to see it end.

---

It was late Saturday night and they were walking back to her car after seeing a movie. They drew a lot of attention whenever they went out in town. People would look at them oddly and Shelby couldn't be certain if they were wondering what she was doing with Sam or why he was with her. The first handful of times it happened, it really bothered her, but now? She was getting used to it.

Sort of.

They were halfway across the parking lot when Mr. and Mrs. Watkins who owned the pharmacy down on First Street walked past them in the opposite direction.

"It's such a shame," Mrs. Watkins whispered loudly enough for Shelby to hear. "I always thought she was such a nice girl."

Sam squeezed her hand but neither acknowledged the comment and simply kept walking. It's what they did now – pretended the comments didn't bother them.

But they did.

And eventually she was going to have to get a backbone and stand up for herself.

Deciding she needed to stop obsessing about it, she let out a long breath and opted for a new topic. "So...I was wondering if you would like to come to church with me tomorrow," she said casually, like she wasn't completely nervous about speaking the suggestion out loud. They were holding hands, walking along like they didn't have a care in the world, and she found herself holding her breath waiting for his response.

"Uh...tomorrow?"

She nodded, doing her best to keep looking forward so she couldn't see the expression on his face. "I'm not helping out in any of the Sunday School classes or in any of the nurseries, so I just thought...I don't know...maybe you would come with me just for the actual sermon part."

"Tomorrow," he said.

Now she did glance over and saw he had a grim look on his face. "Yes. Tomorrow." She paused. "But if you have other plans or if you just don't want to, it's okay. I was thinking it might be nice for you to meet my parents when it's not so one-on-one and there would be plenty of distractions around, but...we can do it some other time. No worries."

"No, I...I didn't say I wouldn't..."

"But..."

He sighed and now they were at the car. Once they were situated and pulling out of the parking lot, he continued. "Do I have to like...dress up or something? Wear a suit? Get a haircut?" Reaching up, he raked his fingers through his hair. "I've been meaning to get it cut but..." Then he shook his head. "I can make sure it doesn't look too bad."

And her heart melted a little right then and there. How adorable was he? Reaching over, she took his hand in hers. "You just have to go and be yourself, Sam. No suit, no haircut, just...you."

He looked at her like he didn't believe her. "Shell, I can't go in jeans and sneakers. I mean...come on."

"Why not? You think you'd be the only one?"

"Seriously?"

She nodded. "We're not an overly formal church, Sam.

There's no dress code. You can dress casually. And besides, it's not what you wear that matters."

Another look of disbelief.

"It's true! Some of the best-dressed people in church can be the biggest hypocrites so don't let them fool you. I learned very young how there are people who look and act a certain way on Sunday mornings and then are completely different Monday through Saturday in the real world. And not in a good way."

He nodded. "Yeah, I've run into people like that. They seem like they're the nicest people in the world – they dress a certain way, speak in a certain tone of voice, but then they show their true colors."

And for some reason, she kind of had a feeling he was referring to specific people.

And not just the Watkins' who just walked by.

Like maybe her parents.

"If you don't want to go..."

Looking over at her, he gave her a small smile. "It's not that. Not really." He paused. "I'm a realist, Shelby. I know what most people think of me and I'd be lying if I said it didn't bother me. A lot of the things I've done were stupid and inconsiderate, but most of them were done out of immaturity. If I could, I'd go back and change them, but I can't. Now I have to live with the consequences."

"That's why you don't want to live here. It's not so much that you resent your great-grandfather putting that clause in his will. It's having the eyes of the town on you."

He nodded.

"And going to church with me tomorrow will sort of amplify that, won't it?"

It wasn't really a question.

He nodded again. "You can't tell me you're okay with it – the looks, the whispering..."

Squeezing his hand, she couldn't help but feel bad for him. She was used to the eyes of the town being on her. Growing up as the pastor's daughter, everyone kept watching and waiting for her to rebel. Any time she did anything anyone deemed "out of line," it got reported to her parents. She understood Sam's feelings, although she was pretty sure nothing she ever did compared to his shenanigans. The worst she'd ever done was break curfew a handful of times and well...dating him. So yeah, she couldn't fully compare the two of them, but she understood the feelings.

And by asking him to come with her to church tomorrow, she was getting that backbone she knew she needed. It would be her way of facing off with the people of the town and saying "Yes, he's with me and if you have something to say, bring it!"

Of course, it all sounded good in her head. The reality could be a lot worse.

For both of them.

Ugh...

"You know what? It's not a big deal. If you want to come with me, great, but if you don't, then that's fine too." She smiled at him. "Seriously, no pressure." And she meant it.

"I'm going to have to meet your parents eventually," he said mildly.

Maybe it was crazy to think that her heart actually skipped a beat at his statement, but it did. By saying those words, it implied he saw this relationship as getting serious.

And that made her brave.

"I lied."

Sam looked over at her. "Excuse me?"

Nodding, she repeated herself. "I lied."

"About what?" His eyes had gone a little wide and he looked mildly worried.

"I really think you should come with me tomorrow," she stated firmly, even as she forced herself not to look at him. It was easier that way. "I think the only way to get everyone to quit whispering and stop with all the judgy looks is to go to the one place where we can face them all at once." Letting out a long breath, she paused and collected her thoughts a bit. "I can't help nor do I condone how some of most judgmental people come to church on Sundays or how most of them are hypocrites, but I think we could do away with a lot of it by going there together."

Now she faced him, holding his hand tightly.

"But only if you're okay with it."

At that point they were pulling into her driveway and Shelby waited for his answer.

And waited.

And waited.

He turned off the car and got out. Shelby followed him to the front door and watched as he unlocked it and then stepped back while she walked in first.

*Okay, he wants to finish the conversation in here. Fine.*

When she turned around to face him, he was walking into the bedroom. Sighing wearily, she followed him and had to wonder if she had pushed a little too much.

And when she found him pulling clothes out of the closet she knew she had.

He was leaving. Going back to his mother's place all because she had gone and made some demands on his time and tried to push him into doing something he clearly didn't want to do. She wouldn't cry – wouldn't allow herself to – not until he left. And really, she didn't even want to be in here while he packed because it hurt too much.

Turning, she walked out of the room and mentally cursed herself. Why would she think that tonight would be the right time to ask such a thing of Sam? Especially after hearing Mrs. Wilkins' comment?

*You're smarter than this, Shelby!*

Obviously, she wasn't.

Walking into the kitchen, she grabbed a bottle of water from the refrigerator and sat down at the table. No doubt Sam would be packed up in about fifteen minutes. It wasn't like he had a lot of things here, but they were scattered all over the house – clothes, shoes, his tablet, phone charger, iPod...okay, maybe he did have a lot of things here, but they could all be packed up relatively quickly.

She heard footsteps coming down the hall and forced herself to sit up straight and listen to him tell her how he was leaving.

*Be brave. You can cry later.*

"Hey, Shell? Which shirt do you think works better – the gray or the navy?" Sam walked into the kitchen carrying two dress shirts on hangers and looking at her with a lopsided grin.

"Um...what?" she croaked, certain she must have misheard him.

"Most of my stuff here is work clothes, but I do have a couple of polo shirts if you don't like either of these." He shrugged and studied the shirts before looking back at her. "I'm not going to wear a tie or anything with them, but I kind of thought these would be okay. What do you think?"

Before she knew it, Shelby flung herself out of her seat and launched herself at him. The shirts fell to the ground as he caught her. With her legs wrapped around his waist, she kissed him soundly. They were both breathless when they broke apart.

"Had I known my shirts did this sort of thing for you, I would have carried them around here every night!" he teased, walking them back to the bedroom. Placing her on the bed, he kissed her again before lifting his head. "So was it the gray or the blue that really threw you over the edge?"

Laughing, Shelby swatted him away. "It wasn't the shirts, you doofus. Although...okay, it kind of was, but not in the way you're thinking."

He lay down on the bed beside her and played with her hair. "Then you need to explain it because I'm thoroughly confused."

Feeling more than a little embarrassed, she confessed about her thinking how he was leaving. "I'm sorry," she said softly. "As I was saying it I realized how that didn't really make either of us sound good – you for being willing to leave over something so small and me for thinking so little of you." She shook her head. "Forgive me?"

Reaching up, Sam caressed her cheek – something he knew she loved when he did. "There's nothing to forgive. I think it's a sensitive subject for both of us but...you're right. We need to face this problem head-on and tell people they can go to hell if they want to gossip about us."

She couldn't help but laugh. "Which would really be fitting should tomorrow's sermon be on how gossip is the work of the devil." Then she laughed even harder and was relieved when Sam joined her.

Then he was stretched out on top of her and they were no longer laughing, but kissing instead. Wrapping her limbs around him, Shelby held him close and it didn't take long before they started to move. Breaths became more ragged as movements became more urgent. In the blink of an eye, she was lying naked beneath him staring up at his heated gaze.

"Do you have any idea what you do to me, Shelby?" he

whispered, his hands roaming over her torso before he boldly cupped her breasts. "Your laughter, your smile...the sweet smell of your skin..." Leaning down, he flicked her nipple with his tongue before looking back at her. "The sounds you make when I touch you..." He groaned sexily. "You're perfect."

She felt herself flushing at the compliment. "I'm hardly that, Sam," she said quietly, raking her hand through his hair. "But I'm glad you think so."

"Always," he said, his voice low and gruff and oh-so-serious. "From the moment I saw you."

"Sam..."

"You don't have to believe me," he said, lowering his head again. "But I know the truth."

And at that point, she would have believed anything he told her because his mouth, hands and body were making her crazy in the best possible way.

And she loved every minute of it.

## 10

It was kind of hard to keep a smile on his face when he could hear so many of the whispered comments all around them.

Most of them weren't particularly nice.

*What's he doing here?*

*I'm surprised he didn't burst into flames walking through the door!*

*Leave it to Sam to try to corrupt the nicest girl in town.*

*You'd think Shelby would know better.*

He was used to them – hell, he'd heard them enough over the years – but he didn't like it for Shelby's sake. Although, she was getting used to it as well, judging by the way their eyes met after each and every comment. She'd look up at him and smile and shrug. It was nice that she wasn't getting upset, but part of him wished she would.

How twisted was that?

Maybe if she got upset about it he would have proof that he wasn't the right guy for her and how she'd be better off without him and with someone else.

Yeah, that was something that had been going through

his mind a lot lately. He'd never felt for someone the way he felt about Shelby and it was more than a little terrifying. Sam had a plan for his life – or at least, he used to have one before he met her. She was turning his life a little upside down and making him second-guess everything he thought he wanted. Being with Shelby meant being here in Magnolia Sound. There was no way he would ever ask her to leave here. This was her home and if he could ever get past his own twisted thoughts on the place, Sam knew it was a place he could call home as well.

If he wanted to.

It just sucked that his natural tendency and his first thought whenever he did think about staying here was to remind himself of all the reasons to leave.

And he only had one reason to stay.

Not counting his family, of course.

Maybe he should talk to his sister about this. She and Jake had struggled with logistics where their relationship was concerned almost since the beginning. The only difference was that Magnolia Sound was always the end-game for them. It was just a matter of timing to get them both here at the same time.

Sam had never wanted to live here.

Beside him, Shelby squeezed his hand and smiled up at him.

And his immediate thought was how he wanted to keep that smile on her face always.

It was a hell of an internal battle.

"Mom, Dad," Shelby said, interrupting his thoughts, "this is Sam Westbrook. My boyfriend."

Sam smiled as he looked at Steve and Caroline Abbott and had to remind himself to breathe. This was it – the moment he had been dreading for years. He was finally face-to-face with the pastor who seemed to know of his every misdeed.

Now he had to remind himself not to throw up.

Shaking each of their hands in turn, Sam said, "It's a pleasure to meet you both." And while Shelby's mother continued to smile at him, Sam noticed her father's smile was one of cool detachment.

Not very pastorly, he thought, but immediately pushed it aside.

"Would the two of you like to join us for lunch?" Caroline asked. "I don't have anything prepared at home, but maybe we can go someplace and…"

"How about Sam and I pick up something and bring it over to your place?" Shelby asked before looking up at Sam. "Would that be all right?"

He nodded but he wasn't completely sure that was the best option. If they went to a restaurant or something, there'd be less chance of some big interrogation from her father. But there was no way he could say that, right?

"We could go to the deli and grab some cold cuts and salads and sit out on the back deck and relax," Shelby went on. "How does that sound?"

When everyone was in agreement, Sam shook both their hands again and stepped back as Shelby hugged her parents before they left. There was no way he could suddenly come up with a reason why he couldn't go to lunch, so he quietly resigned himself to whatever was to come.

It was almost like walking off to his own execution and the worst part was Shelby had no idea just how much he dreaded it. The only positive – if he had to find something – was that maybe things would go exactly as he predicted and he'd be proven right. Her parents would strongly protest this relationship and Shelby would have to end things with him. He knew that would kill him, but at the same time, it was better for it to happen sooner rather than later.

They were in the car and pulling out of the church parking lot when she spoke. "You're being awfully quiet. Are you sure you're okay with this?"

It was like she could read his mind, but there was no way he was going to answer her honestly. "Just nervous," he replied.

"You have nothing to be nervous about," she countered. "It's just lunch and some conversation and I promise we won't stay all day." She paused. "Why don't we go out on the boat later on? It will give us the perfect excuse to leave early. What do you think?"

"That's fine," he murmured, navigating the traffic to get them across town to pick up lunch.

"Sam…"

With a weary sigh, he glanced over at her. "What do you want me to say, Shelby? We both know this has the potential to go horribly wrong. I know we had to do this eventually, but you can't blame me for being a little hesitant about the whole thing. Would you be looking forward to going someplace where you knew you were going to be put under the microscope and everyone knew all the bad things you've ever done?" he asked with a little more heat than he knew she deserved.

"Okay, I get it, but I still think you're blowing it all out of proportion. It's not going to be that bad."

There was no way he was going to argue the point with her because…well…there was no point. Sam knew who he was and he knew the things he'd done and knew what was coming. But if Shelby wanted to be in denial for a little bit longer, he'd let her.

An hour later, it was like sitting and waiting for the bomb to go off.

"Sam, I have to tell you," Caroline began once they were all seated and had said the blessing, "the grounds around town have never looked better! You certainly have a gift!"

Wait...what was happening here?

"Oh, um...thanks," he murmured with a small smile.

"Everything has been such a mess since the hurricane and you've done wonders with the cleanup and making things look so fresh and beautiful again," she said. "We could certainly use some of that around the church grounds."

And there it was.

Sam glanced over at Shelby's father and saw the slight smirk on his face and figured there was no longer a way for him to ignore the topic. "I think the church grounds look fine," he said. "There wasn't any ground damage to it and the crew you have does a great job with keeping it all well-manicured."

"Well," Shelby interjected, "it's not just the existing church grounds but the property behind it. I know we've been waiting years to be able to do something with it, right, Dad?"

Steve nodded but his eyes never left Sam's face.

And yet he didn't utter a word.

Swallowing hard, Sam eyed his sandwich and wished he could just eat. Unfortunately, all three Abbotts were looking at him. "Is there something wrong with the company you're currently using?"

"Earl Bennett is retired and simply looking for something to do," Caroline explained. "He's fine for doing the mowing and trimming the shrubs, but the property in the back requires tree removal and someone with an artistic eye to turn it into a bit of an oasis that meets the church's needs."

She was still smiling as she spoke and Sam had to admit she seemed much nicer up close than she had in the past whenever he'd seen her around town.

Not that it mattered right now because he could tell she had an agenda and wasn't the kind of person who took no for an answer.

*Great.*

"I know we've left several messages with your service about coming in and looking at it," Caroline said with another sweet smile and that's when Sam knew he was doomed.

Carefully he pushed his plate aside and cleared his throat. "With all due respect, Mrs. Abbott, I just don't think I'm the right person for the job." He glanced over at Steve. "I guess I should have just called and said as much sooner and for that I apologize. I can give you the name of another company who would be better suited."

With his appetite gone, Sam contemplated excusing himself and leaving before he embarrassed himself or Shelby any further. But as he was about to push his chair back, Steve spoke.

"Your great-grandfather used to come and handle the property himself at one time," he began pleasantly. "It was when we were just starting out and it was his contribution to the church. He could have sent one of his employees to handle it, but every Saturday morning he would show up and do it himself."

Sam let out a slow breath and braced himself for the speech on what a great man his great-grandfather was and how Sam was nothing like him.

Worst. Lunch. Ever.

"As we grew, he stepped back and let others serve in that capacity. But every once in a while, he'd be the one out there pushing the mower," Steve explained. "I remember stepping outside one Saturday and seeing him there. Ezekiel had to be about eighty at that point and I was stunned to see him. I said 'Zeke, what in the world are you doing?'" He paused and laughed softly. "And do you know what he said to me?"

Sam shook his head.

"He said, 'Old Tom can't mow a straight line so I told him I'd do it this week and show him how it's done.'" He paused and laughed again. "And sure enough, Tom Connors was standing by the front of the church watching Zeke mow! He was only fifty years old and there was Zeke calling him old!"

Sam had to laugh at that too because it was typical of his great-grandfather. He never thought of himself as old but didn't hesitate to call others out on their age. "That sounds just like him, Sir."

Steve's eyes widened slightly before he relaxed. "He used to brag about how talented you were – how you were the only one in the family to inherit his green thumb."

The statement wasn't a surprise because many people had said the same to him, so he simply nodded and waited to see what else Shelby's father had to say.

"I'm not trying to tell you how to run your business, Sam, but it might not hurt to come and take a look at the property," Steve said before picking up his sandwich. He looked across the table at Shelby and smiled. "Thanks for picking up lunch, Shelly Bean."

She gasped and looked anxiously over at Sam as if mortified that her father would use that nickname in front of him. He smirked as he pulled his plate back in front of him and took a bite.

But he knew what he was going to be calling her later on.

---

It was after midnight and Shelby knew she should be asleep, but her mind simply wouldn't shut down.

Lunch with her parents had gone...well.

Kind of.

It was a little eye-opening because she knew how Sam felt and he had warned her of how he felt her parents viewed him, but it wasn't until she was there witnessing for herself that she started to maybe see his side of things.

Her mother was polite – overly so – but she was also very single-minded in her conversation with Sam. And her father? Well, she was used to him being polite and wanting to point out the good in people, but she felt like his conversation about Sam's great-grandfather wasn't so much to point out what an amazing man Ezekiel was as it was a not-so-subtle reminder of how Sam wasn't measuring up.

Conversation had died down after that and they had eaten their meal while making polite small talk about the weather and upcoming church events. No one bothered to ask Sam about his family or about the work his mother was doing on the bed and breakfast and they didn't even ask how the two of them had come to start dating.

Had they always been this way, her parents? Were they simply good at making small talk while silently ignoring the topics that really needed to be discussed?

Turning her head, she looked as Sam slept peacefully beside her. His hair was all disheveled and his jaw was rough with stubble and he was the sexiest thing she had ever seen. He went to lunch today to please her – to make her happy – even though he knew it was going to be awkward, and she had been so determined to prove him wrong that she pushed his feelings aside.

And now she felt awful about it.

After they left her parents, they went out on the boat and laughed and made love and ended the day in a much better manner, but...she still felt bad. Guilty. Like she needed to make things up to him.

Rolling onto her side, Shelby reached out and gently caressed his cheek. She loved the scratchy feel of his skin and when he hummed in his sleep, she found it incredibly sweet.

The thought almost made her laugh because she couldn't imagine anyone thinking of Sam as sweet. But she did. There was so much more to him than people knew, and she wished they would open their minds a little bit and find that out for themselves.

"Why aren't you asleep?" he whispered, turning slightly to kiss her palm.

"I was just lying here thinking," she said softly.

His eyes opened and although it was dark in the room, there was enough moonlight that she could see him blink several times as if bringing her into focus. "I'm sorry I ruined lunch," he said, not for the first time that day.

"You didn't ruin anything," she said, also not for the first time that day. "We've discussed this, Sam."

"And yet you're still up thinking about it."

He had her there.

"It was all just a little...eye-opening, that's all."

Reaching out, Sam pulled her into his embrace and

hugged her close. "Don't think about it anymore, Shelly Bean." They both started to laugh.

"You've been waiting all day to use that, haven't you?" she deadpanned.

"You know it."

She relaxed against him. "I hate that I made you go there, Sam. I made you do something you didn't want to do and made you uncomfortable. It wasn't very nice of me."

He was quiet for so long that she feared he had fallen back to sleep, but then she felt him place a light kiss on her forehead. "Stop thinking and go to sleep."

Even as she closed her eyes, Shelby knew she wasn't ready to sleep just yet. Snuggling in closer, she kissed his chest. "I may need a little help with that." Another kiss. "Maybe you could do something to clear my mind and exhaust me."

For a man half-asleep, he moved pretty fast. Before she knew it, Shelby was pinned beneath him. "Are you saying you want to use sex as a distraction?" he teased lightly.

Wrapping her arms and her legs around him, she met his gaze. "Does that make me a bad person?"

His laugh was low and quickly turned to a growl as she rubbed herself against him. "Damn, Shelby," he groaned, "we should both be asleep right now."

"And we will be," she whispered, leaning up to kiss his skin wherever she could reach. "I promise."

Sam pressed her more firmly into the mattress as he claimed her lips with his. She loved his kisses, craved his kisses, and while she knew this wasn't going to solve anything, there was nothing else in the world she wanted more than what they were doing right now.

"Sam?"

"Hmm?"

"Make love to me," she begged, and as he slowly moved against her she sighed with pleasure and let him do just that until neither of them could keep their eyes open. It was glorious.

―――――

"You know I don't like to pry."

Shelby looked across the table at her mother and forced herself to smile and not react. "I know, Mom."

"But...what exactly are you doing with someone like Sam Westbrook?"

"What do you mean?" Yeah, Shelby had a feeling she knew exactly what her mother meant, but she needed to hear the explanation for herself.

"Shelby, your father and I have introduced you to plenty of nice young men – decent, respectful young men – who you've never shown any interest in. Is this some sort of rebellion?"

"I'm a little old for that, don't you think?"

"What other conclusion could I come to?"

They were eating lunch at the Magnolia Sound Country Club and speaking so politely it was almost as if they were discussing the weather or talking to a stranger. For the first time in her life, Shelby wished she had canceled their lunch date.

Something she only felt mildly guilty about.

For a moment, she fidgeted with her napkin because she had to get her emotions under control. They had never done this – had the kind of conversation where Shelby spoke up for herself. In the past, she had a tendency to cave when she knew her parents disapproved of something. But not this time.

Possibly not ever again.

With a steadying breath, she looked at her mother. "I am dating Sam because he's a good man."

Her mother's soft snort was her only reaction.

Stiffening her spine a bit, she went on. "He's smart, he's funny, he's hard-working, but more than anything else, he likes me for who I am. He *listens* to me," she finished with emphasis.

"Shelby, I'm sure you're flattered because he's paying attention to you. A good-looking, charismatic man like that is something new to you – a novelty."

"Wow," Shelby said with a hint of disgust. "Thanks."

Reaching across the table, Caroline squeezed her daughter's hand. "I'm just saying he's different from any man you've ever dated. You know his reputation and maybe...just maybe...there's a part of you that is looking for acceptance from your peers."

Swiftly pulling her hand back, Shelby stared at her mother in horror. "Do you even hear yourself? Is it possible that Sam and I are together because we genuinely like each other? That there is no ulterior motive?" She let out a long breath. "I am an intelligent and grown woman who is capable of having a relationship with a man my parents didn't choose, which has nothing to do with trying to fit in with the popular crowd, and I resent you even implying such things!"

"Lower your voice, Shelby. You're making a scene," Caroline said in hushed tones as she glanced around the restaurant.

"You know what?" Shelby said, her voice as loud as it was mere seconds ago. "I don't care. We are having a conversation and you just insulted me. You didn't seem to be too concerned how *that* might make a scene."

Shifting in her seat, her mother gave her a sour look. "And this is what happens when you date someone like Sam Westbrook. You've never been disrespectful or argumentative and now you are. I think that speaks volumes for the kind of influence he is."

So many retorts played out in her mind, but there was one question she needed an answer to more.

"If this is how you really feel about Sam, why are you asking him to come do work on the property? Why not just hire someone else and be done with it?"

A small shrug was her only response before Caroline picked up her glass of sweet tea and took a sip.

"Mom?"

Gently placing the glass down, she looked at Shelby. "If it were up to me, we would. Your father is the one insisting on it. I've brought in several landscaping companies and gotten estimates and he refuses to make a decision until he speaks to Sam."

"Why? Why is it so important to him? Is he just hoping to lure Sam into the office so he can ambush him and lecture him on all the ways he's not living a proper life? Is he going to preach to him about all the ways he needs to redeem himself?"

"Well, someone certainly should..."

And that was it. Pushing away from the table, Shelby stood and tossed her napkin down. "We're done here." And surprisingly, her mother didn't try to stop her – no doubt because she didn't want to make a scene. With her head held high, she made her way across the room and out the front door without stopping to speak or even make eye contact with anyone. Her heart was beating so hard that it was painful, but she had to get to her car and get away before she could stop to calm down.

Five minutes later, she felt like she could finally take a breath. There was still time left in her lunch hour and she had barely eaten more than a couple of bites of food, but her appetite was gone. The best thing to do was to go back into the library and try to distract herself. Keeping busy was the most logical solution.

Unfortunately, she didn't feel like being logical.

Something about standing up for herself made her feel brave – and a little sick – but she knew it wasn't only her mother that she had to deal with. All the books in the world weren't going to be distraction enough. She needed to speak to her father and find out what exactly was going on in his head and what his reasoning was for wanting Sam to work for him – or why it was so important to get Sam to give him an estimate on the work.

Pulling her phone from her purse she called the library and was relieved when Laney answered the phone. "Hey, it's me."

"Hey! What's up?"

"I'm going to be late coming back from lunch." Then she paused. "Actually, I'm not sure I'll be back today."

"Are you all right? Are you sick?"

"No. I just had a very stressful conversation with my mother…"

"Been there."

"And now I feel like I need to go have a conversation with my father."

"Why?"

"It's a long story."

"But it's about Sam, right?"

It would be pointless to deny it. "Yes."

She heard Laney sigh. "Go do what you have to do,

Shell. But if you do decide to come back in, can you do me a favor?"

"Sure!"

"Bring coffee and brownies because we're going to need to sit and talk about it."

Smiling, Shelby said, "Deal."

Once her phone was back in her purse, she pulled out of the parking lot and headed toward the church. Her father would be in his office and Shelby knew her mother had a weekly nail appointment on Wednesdays and wouldn't be back any time soon. She used to think it was nice how her parents worked together, but now it wasn't particularly working in her favor. Hopefully her mother wouldn't feel the need to come here and talk to her father so she'd have time to say what she needed to say without an audience.

As she drove down Main Street, she thought about all the things she wanted to ask her father. Everything Sam-related and then – if she could make herself – she wanted to ask if he shared her mother's insulting beliefs about why Shelby and Sam were dating.

"I really hope he doesn't," she murmured.

In her heart, she really hoped her father would be just as appalled by her mother's statements as Shelby was but right now, she couldn't be sure. This was all uncharted territory for them and just as she couldn't have predicted the things her mother said, it was the same for her father.

Putting her directional on, she turned into the church parking lot and found it to be mostly deserted. She spotted her father's car, the cleaning lady's car, and...

Sam's white pickup.

11

It DIDN'T MATTER how many pep talks he had with himself, Sam couldn't stop the slight tremble of his hand as he reached out to knock on Steve Abbott's office door.

He was surprised to see that his wife wasn't sitting at her desk, but maybe that worked to his advantage.

"Come in!" Steve called out pleasantly and didn't seem to be the least bit surprised when Sam walked in. "Hey, Sam! How are you today?"

Clearing his throat mildly, Sam nodded. "I'm good, Sir. Thank you. And you?"

Sitting behind his desk, Steve smiled as he studied him. After a bit of a pause, he replied, "I'm well. Thank you for asking. Won't you have a seat?" He motioned to the chairs in front of his desk and Sam had no choice but to sit. "So what brings you here today?"

Seriously? Where did he even begin?

"I thought I'd come by and see about the property, Sir," he said. "We can walk around and you can tell me what it is you envision for it. You know, if you have the time."

Looking beyond relaxed in his chair, Steve continued to study him.

Wordlessly.

It was so quiet it was awkward.

Clearing his throat again, Sam continued, "I don't know if you already have plans drawn up or if you have any particular designs you want to incorporate, but whatever it is, I can have a full estimate to you by tomorrow."

Nothing.

Doing his best not to appear flustered or frustrated, he added, "If this isn't a good time, I can come back." He looked over his shoulder toward the reception area. "I see Mrs. Abbott isn't here, but maybe she can call and let me know when you have an opening in your schedule."

Then, Steve stood and walked around the desk toward Sam until he was standing in front of him. Arms crossed, he leaned against the desk and stared down at him. "We've been leaving messages for you for weeks now. What changed your mind about coming in?"

"Honestly?"

Steve nodded.

"Because it was the right thing to do. It was rude of me not to return your calls and after speaking with you and your wife at lunch on Sunday, I realized just how disrespectful it was."

"You didn't realize that before?"

Sam had to stifle a chuckle because it seemed out of character for a pastor to be sarcastic.

But he kept his observation to himself.

With a small shrug he replied, "I knew it was wrong, but I kept telling myself it was okay and that I was busy."

"And you weren't?"

And now he had to stifle the urge to roll his eyes. "No,

Sir. I wasn't. I mean, I'm busy – this business certainly keeps me working long hours – but not so busy that I didn't have time to return a phone call, so...I'm sorry."

A slow smile spread across Steve's face as he lowered his arms and stepped away from the desk. "Let's go for a walk, shall we?"

For a minute, Sam wasn't sure what to do but when he turned his head and saw the pastor standing in the doorway, he immediately got up and walked out of the office with him. And for the next hour, they walked around and discussed the kind of project that practically had Sam salivating. It would involve letting him design and get creative with the soil – something he loved to do. Steve was open to his suggestions and for a little while, he forgot to be nervous. He wasn't dealing with the local pastor or Shelby's father, he was dealing with a potential client who seemed impressed with Sam's knowledge.

Besides talking about the project, they shared funny stories about Ezekiel and some of their shared interests here in Magnolia, like sailing and fishing. If they didn't have a negative history – and Sam was willing to concede that he was fully to blame there – he would have thoroughly enjoyed himself and perhaps even considered Steve a friend.

He even talked about the trouble he was having getting to get the good people of Magnolia to see him as the man he was rather than the rebellious teen he had been, and Steve actually had some insightful advice for him.

"You know, Sam, the best way is to keep showing them the man you are now. You're hard-working and a trustworthy businessman. If Ezekiel trusted you with his business, that should speak volumes to the folks around here. Your great-grandfather owned a lot of businesses and he had a lot of grandchildren and great-grandchildren – most of whom didn't inherit businesses. I think that says a lot."

Yeah, Sam had thought of that too. Other than Sam and Mallory, most of his cousins received their college educations or trust funds. Mason never mentioned what Pops left him and he knew he'd get it out of him sooner or later, but… it certainly did put a new perspective on things.

Go figure.

Perhaps Steve wasn't such a bad guy after all.

They were at the back door of the church when Steve stopped and faced him. "Can I ask you something?"

He nodded.

"Why the church?"

Frowning, he asked, "Excuse me?"

"I mean, for all of your antics, why the church? Why was *this* the place you felt like you had to come and raise hell?" Then he chuckled. "Sorry, bad choice of words, but I think you get my point."

And for some reason, that small joke made Sam relax a bit. "To be honest, Sir, it was pure stupidity."

Steve's eyes went a little wide at the admission.

"It seemed like the ultimate rebellion," he explained. "Not toward you – not really – but it really felt like that in my young mind."

"And the incident three months ago?"

Right then he wished the pavement would open up and swallow him because he couldn't blame immaturity on that particular act. He could feel his cheeks heat and he looked away. "Yeah, um…I have no excuse for that."

"It was disrespectful." But there was no condemnation in his words.

All Sam could do was nod.

"Here's the thing, Sam," Steve began carefully, "I

understand rebellion and I understand that people make poor decisions and make mistakes. I believe in giving people second chances."

And not for the first time, Sam felt like this was a good decision that he came here today.

"However..."

Dammit, he got his hopes up too soon.

"I'm not comfortable with you dating my daughter."

And there it was.

Finally.

"You see, Shelby is a quiet girl. A respectful girl. And Magnolia Sound is her home." He paused. "Word around town is that you're not looking to stay here – you're merely fulfilling the wishes of your great-grandfather. And while I can appreciate that and I think it's admirable what you're doing, we both know your time here is temporary. I'm not keen on the idea of you killing time with my daughter."

Rage slowly began to simmer within him, but Sam knew he had to tread carefully because at the end of the day, this man was still Shelby's father and he needed to treat him with a measure of respect.

"With all due respect, Sir, Shelby is a grown woman and our relationship isn't anyone's business but ours."

The serene smile on Steve's face never wavered. "I respectfully disagree. She's my daughter and everything about her is my business."

"So you're saying I'm good enough to hire to work for you, good enough that the people around town should give me a second chance, but not good enough for Shelby. Do I have that right?"

"You're over-simplifying it."

"Am I?" he demanded. "Because that's exactly what you're saying. You may try to dress it up with giving me a little praise before insulting me, but the end result is still the same."

"Why don't we go back inside and talk a little more?" Steve suggested.

"Why? I think you've made your stance abundantly clear. You talked a good game about understanding and giving people the benefit of the doubt and second chances, but it seems like you also believe in being selective as to when you actually put those practices into play. And if you think giving me the job is some sort of consolation prize for breaking up with Shelby then you're crazy!"

"I didn't know about your relationship when I reached out to you about the project, Sam. One has nothing to do with the other."

"But you have to admit that – all things considered – it's really a moot point now. There's no way I would work for you knowing how you really feel about me, and if I continue to date your daughter, we both know you'll never give me the job." He turned and started to walk away, but quickly turned back. "You know, Shelby told me what a kind man you were. A fair man. She spoke so highly of you that I almost believed her. But you're not. You're no different than anyone else in this town. It's as if none of you have ever made a mistake. Well let me tell you something, you're judgmental and rude and if you cared about your daughter at all, you'd maybe ask her what it is that makes *her* happy – or who – rather than thinking that you know best."

"Sam..."

"It seems to me that it's your way or no way," he went on. "If someone doesn't live by your rules, then you don't think they're good enough! And you know what? Shelby deserves to choose who she wants to date without your input! She's more than just the preacher's daughter!"

"Is that why you pursued her? Was that one more act of rebellion?" Steve asked and this time he didn't bother to hide the disdain.

For a minute, Sam was too stunned to speak. He knew they were no longer candy-coating anything, but for some reason, he didn't expect the man to hit below the belt.

And since the gloves were clearly off...

"You're a hypocrite, Pastor Abbott," he said with disgust. "You can stand up in front of your congregation and preach about forgiveness and second chances but clearly that only applies to others and not yourself. You speak in your Sunday morning voice even as your words are filled with hate. Shame on you." Taking a few steps back, Sam looked at the building as a whole. "Shame on all of you."

This time when he turned to walk away, he kept going until he was at his truck. So many thoughts raced through his head and unfortunately, there wasn't a damn thing he could do right now. He wanted to punch something or throw something – he wanted to yell and scream and shout profanities...but he'd wait until he was off church property and on the main road.

He paused when he spotted Shelby standing by the front of the building. Muttering a curse, he knew he couldn't just leave. She had spotted him and was currently walking his way.

"Hey!" she said, smiling as she came in close and kissed him. "What are you doing here?"

Raking a hand through his hair, he took a step back. "I um...I just came to talk to your father about the property. You know, the whole park thing."

She frowned and Sam knew she could tell he was tense. "Did it go okay?"

How could he possibly explain it to her? How could he

possibly tell her that her father was a total hypocrite? There was no way he could. Sam always knew his own father's shortcomings and witnessed them firsthand. Shelby didn't grow up that way. She loved and respected her father and he couldn't do anything to jeopardize their relationship.

"It went fine," he said vaguely and forced himself to smile. "I didn't know you were going to be here. Shouldn't you be back at the library?" This time she was the one to fidget and he stopped focusing on himself and saw how uncomfortable she looked. "Is everything all right?" He reached for her hand and tugged her in close.

"I had a fight with my mother at lunch and now I need to go and talk to my dad."

It was on the tip of his tongue to make a snide comment, but he didn't. Hurting Shelby wasn't the thing to do right now. She needed to be comforted. "Want to talk about it with me? I'm a good listener."

As she sagged against him and wrapped her arms around his waist, she sighed. "Thank you, but this is something I need to take care of with him directly." She paused and looked up at him. "Are you free for dinner later?"

He should say no – there was too much going on in his head and maybe some time apart would help – but he couldn't make himself say it. "How about Chinese food and a movie at home?"

"Sounds perfect. Thank you." Then she kissed him and walked away.

And Sam knew he was going to have to start getting used to that last part.

Soon.

"Shelby? What are you doing here?"

Frowning, she stepped into her father's office and thought that – for the first time ever – he didn't seem pleased to see her. His expression was a little tight and he looked tense.

So maybe Sam lied and their meeting hadn't gone all that well.

*Great.*

Hoping to hold onto some of her bravado, she stepped into the office and closed the door behind her. The curious look her father gave her showed he wasn't expecting that. "I just saw Sam out front." And maybe it was her imagination, but her father seemed to pale.

"Did you?"

She nodded.

"What did he have to say?"

"I'd like to hear how you thought it went," she countered, standing in front of the desk.

"Shelly bean, why don't you sit down? You look very uncomfortable standing there."

"I'm fine."

With a weary sigh, he said, "Sam showed up here without an appointment and we went out and walked the property. He had some wonderful ideas and gave me some suggestions and he understands our vision for the park."

Doing her best to keep her expression neutral, she asked, "So you hired him?"

Steve was silent for a moment and began shuffling papers around on his desk. "He still has to give us an estimate."

"But you're going to hire him?"

This time he looked directly at her. "Shelby, what are

you doing with that man? He's not someone you should be involved with."

And there it was, she thought. It wasn't just her mother thinking those things. It was both of them, so any hope of finding an ally here were officially crushed.

"I didn't ask for your advice on my relationship with Sam, Dad. I'm asking about this project. Are you going to hire him?"

Straightening in his seat, he replied, "No. No, I don't think I am."

For a minute she was too stunned to speak. "Then why? Why were you pursuing him? I don't think it had anything to do with me because it sounds like you started reaching out to him before we got involved, so what kind of game are you playing?"

"I don't appreciate the accusation, young lady."

"And I don't appreciate knowing that this is how you treat someone."

Steve got to his feet, but Shelby didn't feel intimidated. Sure, her heart was beating like mad once again and she felt herself begin to tremble, but she wasn't going to back down.

"If you had no intention of hiring him, why did you pursue him?" she demanded.

"You've got this all wrong, Shelby, and when we're done I'm going to expect an apology," he said calmly. "I always intended to hire Sam – and not just because of my friend-ship with Ezekiel, but because he does good work."

Okay, now she was mildly confused.

"I understand teen rebellion and people making bad choices, you know that," he explained. "And Sam and I even discussed that when he showed up here earlier."

"O-kay..."

"We actually had a very pleasant conversation. He's

very smart and he certainly knows a lot about horticulture and working with the land."

"Then I don't understand why you won't hire him."

The smile her father gave her was one of mild condescension. "He turned me down."

"What?"

He nodded. "That's right. He turned me down. Said he wouldn't work for me." He paused. "I'm not surprised, Shelby. A man like that...well...he can't be trusted."

"You just said you thought he did good work," she argued.

"His work isn't in question, it's who he is as a person. This project would be good for him and good for the community, but he couldn't put his personal opinion of me aside." He shrugged. "Now tell me, is that the kind of man you think you should be in a relationship with? Someone so unforgiving?"

"I...that's not..."

As he sat back down, he seemed to relax. "How was lunch with your mother?"

Oh, right. That.

"It was fine," she murmured, reaching for the chair behind her and sitting. "We um...we had a bit of a disagreement."

"Really?"

She nodded and then launched into the conversation they had had. "It seems you both don't think very highly of Sam as a person."

"Actions speak louder than words, sweetheart," he said softly. "I think you should consider what others know, Shelby. Right now, you're maybe just a little...dazzled by Sam. But at the end of the day you can't dispute the truth that's right in front of you."

And something about his words rubbed her the wrong way. Leaning forward in her seat, her gaze narrowed. "So that's it? You're just writing him off? Sam Westbrook doesn't deserve forgiveness? He doesn't warrant a second chance or to have someone maybe give him the benefit of the doubt?"

"That's not what I'm saying..."

"It's exactly what you're saying!" she cried, jumping to her feet. "I've never known you to be so close-minded!" And then it hit her, and she gasped softly.

"Shelby?"

"It's me, isn't it? Your problem with Sam is about me."

His expression never wavered, but his silence spoke volumes.

"You would have given him the job and recommended him to everyone in town. He's good enough to work for you but not good enough to date your daughter."

More silence.

"That's why Sam turned you down, isn't it?" It wasn't a question. "You told him as much and that's why he left."

"He refused to see reason."

"You're lying," she said tightly.

"I am many things, Shelby, but I am not a liar and I resent you saying that. You need to apologize."

But she was stepping away from her seat and making her way toward the office door. Before she could reach it, her mother opened it and stepped in.

"Steve, you aren't going to believe..." Caroline paused as she noticed her daughter. "Shelby? What are you doing here? I thought that was your car out in the lot, but shouldn't you be back at the library?"

"I took the afternoon off," she said as unease wrapped around her.

"That's not very responsible of you," her father admonished. "And it's not fair to your co-workers either. I hope you arranged for coverage."

"This is no doubt *his* influence," her mother added as if Shelby wasn't even in the room. "I knew this would happen."

"That is enough!" Shelby snapped. "I am not going to stand here and listen to any more of this! You know, the two of you had the ability to help Sam – to show him some grace – and instead you chose to be no different than everyone else. You had the opportunity to lead by example and truly extend some grace. But you didn't and I'm disappointed in both of you!"

She noticed the panicked look between her parents and knew she had to leave before things got worse. Without a word, she fled the room and made her way quickly out of the church as tears stung her eyes. How had the day gone so wrong? How had her life gotten so complicated?

She looked around frantically and hoped Sam was still around but he wasn't. Should she call him? Go and find him? Go back to work? She was completely conflicted and hurting and the real problem was...the one person she wanted to comfort her was the reason for all of it.

Knowing she had to go, she got in the car and drove back to the library. Maybe Laney would be able to talk her off of the ledge. She didn't remember leaving the parking lot and she certainly didn't remember the drive across town but suddenly she found herself walking through the front door of the library.

"No coffee? No brownies?" Laney teased, her hand over her heart. "I'm offended." But she immediately sensed something was wrong and called out to Julie to watch the front desk. Scurrying around to Shelby, she led her back to the break room and shut the door. "What happened?" she asked softly, guiding her onto the sofa. "Are you okay?"

For the next ten minutes, Shelby rambled on about the events of the day and the conversation with both her parents and Sam. Tears streamed down her face and when she was done speaking, she had to force herself to breathe and calm down. Looking over at Laney, she asked, "Am I crazy?"

"Why would you even think that?"

"Because it seems like everyone is saying it! We walk around town and people whisper about how crazy it is that Sam and I are together. My parents are completely against us." She paused and wiped her eyes. "And even I thought it was crazy to get involved with Sam! I mean, all the signs are pointing to it, Laney! All Sam wants is to fly under the radar here in town and dating me has done the exact opposite for him and now...now it's costing him work!"

With a snort, Laney reached over for some napkins and handed them to Shelby. "Please, you're not costing him anything. I don't know Sam so I can't say for certain, but he seems to have crews working all over this town, Shell. So what if he doesn't do this job for your dad? If you ask me, that's your father's loss, not Sam's."

"Maybe."

Taking one of Shelby's hands in hers, Laney squeezed it. "Shell, you can't let other people's opinions keep you from being happy! *That* would make you crazy!"

"But how can I keep going like this? I don't want to fight with my parents and it's obvious they don't like Sam, so what am I supposed to do?"

"Your folks will have to get over it. I mean...this thing with Sam...you're serious about him, aren't you?"

She nodded.

"Are you willing to fight for him? Do you love him?"

Her head began to spin and she felt like she was going to be sick. It was all too much. Were relationships supposed to be this hard? She looked over at her friend helplessly. "I'm not strong enough for this," she said quietly. "One argument with my folks and I'm a mess. I knew things would be a little awkward between Sam and my parents, but I never thought it would be like this. Not ever."

"It will get better," Laney said fiercely. "You have to believe that."

"Yeah, well...maybe it won't. You didn't see the way Sam looked when I saw him in the parking lot. I know he was trying to look and sound calm, but I knew something was up." Resting her head back against the sofa, she sighed. "He told me from the beginning how he didn't like it here – how the people of Magnolia treated him, and I didn't want to believe it. And now I can't believe my own parents are the worst offenders."

For a long moment, Laney simply stared at her. "Can I say something without you freaking out?"

"You mean more than I already am?"

Nodding, she said, "Yeah."

"Might as well. It's not like this day can get any worse."

"Look, we've been friends forever and I've spent a lot of time with you and your parents and...there have been plenty of times when they've been less than...shall we say... gracious toward people."

"What do you mean?"

"I mean I've heard them say things to our friends and even some of the guys you've dated that weren't exactly nice." She let out a long breath. "They use that tone of voice that intimidates people and they come off sounding righteous and...I don't know...I can't imagine it was easy for Sam to stand there and listen."

Shelby stared at her friend in horror. "Have they ever... did they...you know...talk like that to you?"

Laney's expression turned sad. "A time or two. Back in high school. They thought I was a little too wild for you and they said if I wanted the right to come back into their home I would need to calm down and get my life in order."

"*What?*"

She nodded again. "It was the summer I put the blue streak in my hair and wore the Daisy Dukes out on the boat with them."

"Oh good grief..."

"Exactly."

"I'm so sorry, Laney. I really am. I'm so embarrassed!" she cried, covering her face with both her hands.

Laney immediately pulled them away. "Why? You didn't do anything wrong! This is on them! And if you want my opinion, I think it's about time people stood up to them!"

Shelby tried to speak but couldn't think of a thing to say.

"They're basically good people, Shell. They really are. It's just that sometimes they come across as a little...high and mighty. Like the kind of people who think they're better than everyone else."

They sat in silence for several minutes as Shelby's mind whirled.

"So what are you going to do?"

"We're supposed to have dinner together tonight so...I guess we'll talk about it then."

They sat in silence for several minutes before Laney spoke again. "You know, you never answered me."

"About what?"

"Do you love him?"

Tears sprang back into her eyes and all she could do was nod.

Then Laney's arms were around her as she let herself cry. Shelby had no idea how long she cried or even how long they were back in the room. She had lost track of time somewhere around the time when she walked out of the country club earlier. But when she finally pulled herself together, she knew there was no way she could go back to work.

"Please don't hate me..."

"Oh, stop. Go home and just...forget about this day. Take a bubble bath, relax, turn on some music and just let yourself unwind."

"That does sound good."

"Have dinner with Sam and maybe don't talk about what happened today," Laney suggested.

"What? Why? Isn't that counter-productive to what needs to happen?"

Laney shook her head. "You'll have to talk about it eventually, but not tonight. Maybe tonight you just...turn off the rest of the world."

And that sounded even better.

An idea sprang to mind and she felt herself begin to smile. Reaching out, she hugged Laney and thanked her before running out of the library and into her car. By the time she got home, she was practically giddy. It wouldn't solve anything and it was merely prolonging the inevitable, but she felt both she and Sam deserved it.

First, she did as Laney suggested and it was amazing what a good bubble bath could do. Next, she walked around and straightened up the place while listening to some soft music. She pulled out every candle she owned and set them up strategically around the house. Then she texted Sam and asked if he could leave work early – like possibly right now. Holding her phone in her hands, she was practically holding her breath as she waited for his response.

**What about dinner? Should I still pick it up on the way?**

Smiling, she texted him back to tell him no and that they could call it in later.

**I'll be there in 30.**

Now there was a very good chance he was dreading coming over because she was being a little cryptic, but she would hopefully be able to change his mind relatively quickly.

With nothing left to do, Shelby walked back into her bedroom and changed out of her yoga pants and t-shirt and into the lingerie she had been saving for a special occasion. It was white and lacey and barely covered anything on her, but she knew Sam would appreciate it. Covering herself with a short pink satin robe, she did a last check of her hair and makeup before walking around and lighting candles.

Which took way longer than she thought.

No sooner had she lit the last one than she heard Sam's truck pull into her driveway.

Peering out the window, she could see he looked tired, a little dirty from the day, and a whole lot defeated. Her heart ached for him but it was all the more reason for her to do what she was doing. He knocked on the door as he opened it, and she slowly let out a breath as he stepped inside.

"Shelby, I..." His words seemed to die in his throat when he took in what she was wearing. She struck a provocative pose and smiled sexily at him. "What...I mean..." He looked over his shoulder and did his best to fill the doorway so anyone passing by couldn't see her.

How sweet was that?

"I'm so glad you're here," she said a little breathlessly. Reaching out, she tugged him into the house and slammed the door behind them.

"Shelby, what's gotten into you? You can't stand in the doorway half-naked and..."

"That wasn't half-naked," she said with a sweet grin and then dropped the robe to the floor. "This is."

He looked ready to lunge for her but stopped himself. "I'm filthy..."

And for some reason, that was even more of a turn on.

Stepping in close, she gazed up at him. "I know. I like it."

"Shelby..."

But there was no stopping her. Going up on her tiptoes, she wrapped her arms around him and kissed him with everything she had – all the anger and frustration of the day topped with her never-ending need for him. He didn't react at first – didn't touch her.

Pulling back, she said, "I want your dirty hands on me, Sam. Please." And for the briefest moment she thought he was going to reject her, but she licked her lips and that seemed to hit the launch button for him. The next thing she knew, she was in his arms and over his shoulder as he stormed toward the bedroom.

## 12

"IT's a little early for you, isn't it?"

Sam looked over his shoulder and saw his sister climbing up the stairs to the party deck on the family's boathouse. It was early – barely seven o'clock in the morning – but...here he was. He'd left Shelby sleeping and snuck out.

Something he'd never done to her before.

And he felt shitty about it.

He'd gotten up and quietly walked around the house collecting all of his things because he knew it would be harder if she were awake and watching him.

Mallory walked over and sat down on the chaise lounge beside him. "I love this time of day," she said, cradling her travel mug in her hands. "The sun is just coming up, it's cold and brisk out, and the Sound is so calm and peaceful." She paused and took a sip of her coffee. "Plus, things are finally starting to bloom again. It's beautiful."

"Yup."

She glanced over at him and studied him. "Want to talk about it?"

He let out a long breath. "I'm leaving."

Mallory's face showed little to no reaction. "I figured as much."

That surprised him a bit. "Really? How?"

She shrugged. "You're here under protest – you've been saying it for months. Plus, I know you better than anyone else alive. Maybe it's a twin thing but I could tell you were getting restless and knew it was only a matter of time before you packed up and went back to Virginia." Her tone was light and casual and for some reason, it bothered him.

"You don't know me *that* well, Mal," he argued lightly, taking a sip of his own coffee.

"We both know that's not true," she said mildly. "What about Shelby?"

"What about her?"

"Are you going to keep seeing her – do the long-distance thing – or is that over?"

"It's over." It was the most painful thing he ever had to say. The only problem was...Shelby didn't know. They had made love like animals on and off all night, until neither could move or breathe. But when the sex fog lifted, he knew what they were doing – what they were both doing – and it didn't sit well with him. There was no way he was going to come between Shelby and her parents. Knowing his own personal track record, he knew it would be best for him to walk away now before things got any more intense.

Mallory was watching him and he forced himself to look out at the Sound. "Well damn. That makes me sad," she said after a minute. "I thought you were good for each other."

"Yeah, well...that makes one of you."

"Sam..."

He shrugged. "It's true, Mal. Everywhere we went

people commented on how we shouldn't be together – how I was no good for her. It's better this way."

"Better for who?"

"Shelby."

"And what about you? Aren't you entitled to be happy?"

"Apparently not in this town."

"It doesn't have to be like that," she said quietly.

"You haven't been walking around town with me lately. And you weren't there when the good ol' pastor told me I wasn't good enough for his daughter."

"What?" she cried. "When was this?"

Sam relayed the story about his lunch with the Abbotts and then his meeting with Steve the day before. "I'm not going to come between Shelby and her parents. That's not right. And honestly, Mal, it would just be better for everyone if I left."

"I disagree."

"Surprise, surprise," he murmured, taking another sip of his own coffee.

"This is where Pops wanted you to be! It's where Mom wants you to be! And it's where I want you to be! Don't you get it?"

"Pops was wrong," he said, but the words felt wrong coming out of his mouth. "He didn't do this for me; he did it for him – so he could try to control one last thing."

"You're wrong," Mallory said vehemently. "He loved you and he wanted to do something that would make you happy."

"Forcing me to be someplace I don't belong isn't making me happy, Mal!" he yelled. "Don't you get it?"

"Why are you like this? Why are you so angry about being given such an incredible gift? You weren't doing anything great back in Virginia, Sam! You have the chance to do something great here! You have a business – a thriving business! Why would you throw that away?"

"I don't know why you're surprised," he griped. "Everyone knows I'm a screw-up."

"No, you're not! I know that, Mom knows it, and Pops knew it!"

He stayed silent for several minutes and tried hard to swallow the lump of emotion clogging his throat. "I'm mad at him for dying – for leaving before I could prove to him that I could change. He was always so disappointed in me and I hate how his last thoughts of me were that he had to save me because I couldn't save myself." He paused. "He didn't think I could make it on my own. And apparently, he was right."

"That's not true, Sam. You need to stop thinking like that!"

"Hard to argue with what's right in my face," he said, his voice low and gruff. "I'm not going to lie to you. I'm a little disappointed too. I had all kinds of plans and ideas for ways to grow the business and once the town is finally cleaned up from all the storm damage, I totally envisioned ways to spruce up some of the properties – including this one. But it's just not meant to be."

"But it can be! Why are you so willing to give up?" Mallory sat up beside him and faced him. "You aren't a quitter, Sam!"

"Unfortunately, Mal, I am. I always have been. I go from job to job and place to place. And do you know why?" He didn't wait for her answer. "Because I'm a quitter. Sorry to disappoint you."

Her expression was fierce and he knew she had a dozen retorts at the ready, and she was showing great restraint by staying silent.

"I'm going to call Mason later on today and talk to him to let him know he's inheriting a landscaping business."

"You know that's not what he wants either. He's got enough issues with being forced to live a life dictated to him by other people. Are you sure you want to add to that? I thought you guys were friends now."

"We are," Sam replied mildly. "He can sell the business if he doesn't want to run it. Then he'd have some cash to maybe get away from here and do something he wants. So, if you think about it, I'm helping him."

"Oh, good grief," she groaned. "That is the most warped logic I've ever heard."

Sam knew she didn't realize it, but he was sacrificing a lot for the people he loved. And yeah, he was in love with Shelby. In the long run, his leaving would ensure her happiness. She could walk around town without people whispering about her and she'd find a respectable guy her parents approved of and live happily ever after.

Without him.

Which pretty much gutted him.

And as much as it was really an afterthought, he would be helping his cousin and God knew he needed the help. So while everyone would look at him as a loser and a quitter, Sam knew he was doing the right thing.

Maybe in time others would see it that way too.

Beside him, Mallory stood up and looked down at him sadly. "You disappoint me."

He let out a mirthless laugh. "I disappoint everyone, Mal. Tell me something I don't know."

"Please don't do this," she said quietly. "Don't walk away. Prove everyone wrong."

Looking up at her, he smiled sadly. "Believe it or not, in the long run, I am." He stood up and placed his coffee down on the small table between their chairs and hugged her. "I know you always saw this place as your dream come true, but...it's not like that for everyone. It can't be. And for as much as we're twins and are so much alike, this is one area where we're not."

"I refuse to believe that," she said sadly, hugging him tightly. "I was really looking forward to both of us living here and starting families."

"You've got Peyton and Parker and Mason to do that with." He pulled back and smiled down at her. "And I'll come back and visit from time to time. I promise."

There were tears in his sister's eyes and he hated that he was the one to put them there.

And hated even more that later on today he was going to do the same to Shelby.

Life wasn't fair.

At least, his life wasn't.

Mallory stepped back and sighed. "I hope you'll find your happiness, Sam. If it's not here in Magnolia with your family or with Shelby, then...somewhere. No one deserves it more."

He let out another mirthless laugh. "The universe would disagree."

She leaned in close one last time. "Then maybe it's up to you to prove it wrong."

---

Shelby didn't take it as a good sign when she woke up alone.

But the look on Sam's face when he showed up at her house later that day told her what she already feared.

It was over.

*They* were over.

He didn't kiss her hello and when he simply walked in and sat down on the sofa, Shelby wasn't sure what she was supposed to do. Her only option was to sit and wait to hear what he had to say and hope she didn't make a fool out of herself.

*You did that last night when you thought seducing him would solve some of your problems.*

"I never meant to hurt you," he said quietly, studying his hands with his head bowed. "Part of me thought things wouldn't be this hard – that people wouldn't be so..." He stopped and finally looked at her. "You don't deserve all of the shit that goes along with being with me, Shelby."

"Have I ever complained?" she asked, her voice trembling. "Have I ever once said to you that it bothered me?"

"No. But you should have because I saw it in your face so many times." She saw him swallow hard and it gave her some comfort that this seemed to be just as hard on him as it was on her. "You have a good life here and you have a family who...cares about you, and we both know I am not the man they want for you."

"It's not their decision," she whispered, unable to make herself speak up. Any minute she was going to start to cry and she really didn't want Sam to see that.

His dark eyes looked tortured. "I agree, but we both know if we keep doing what we're doing, it's going to put a strain on your relationship and I don't want to be the cause of that. I refuse to, Shelby. You mean too much to me for me to let that happen."

"You're not the cause, Sam. They are!"

But he shook his head. "No, it's me. Trust me. It's always me."

And that simple statement broke her heart. Didn't he realize his own worth? How amazing he was? Unable to stop herself, Shelby went and sat beside him, clasping his hands in hers. "It's not you, Sam. You are the victim of a group of people who are refusing to learn who you are now because they're fixating on the boy you once were! Don't let them win! You have so much to give – not just here in Magnolia, but in general! To your friends, your family…to us!"

"Shelby…"

One hand reached out and cupped his face. "I love the man that you are, Sam Westbrook. Don't you know that? I am so glad I got to know you – that I didn't just listen to the gossip and that I actually took the time to talk to you and see beyond all of that. You are more than those rumors!"

He blinked at her several times and if she wasn't mistaken, his eyes were bright with unshed tears. "Not everyone is like you, Shelby," he said gruffly as he removed her hand from his face. "The world would be a much better place if they were." Leaning in, he placed a soft kiss on her cheek before he stood up.

"Please don't go," she said as the first tear fell, and she cursed her own weakness.

"It's for the best. Now you'll at least have a chance to be happy and keep your family together."

As he walked to the door, she got up and followed him. "We can get through this, Sam! In time my folks will get to know you and see just how incredible you are!"

One hand was on the doorknob as he looked over his shoulder at her. "They're not interested in that and I'm not interested in jumping through hoops to prove myself. It's not fair to you and it's not fair to me. I can't keep trying to meet everyone's expectations because it's never going to be enough. I'm never going to be the man they want for you."

He paused and pulled the door open. "Take care, Shelby. Be happy."

And then he was gone.

Crumbling to the floor, she let the tears fall. She wanted to scream and howl and tell the world how much she hurt – how she felt like she was dying – but what would be the point? No one seemed to care about her feelings. She was alone and was always going to be alone and right now that was her fate and she was going to embrace it.

Curled up in the fetal position, she cried for all she could have had and all she had lost. She cried at the unfairness of the situation and she cried for how Sam didn't believe he was worthy of love or acceptance.

But more than anything, she cried because he didn't respond to her declaration of love and maybe that said it all right there. He didn't feel for her what she felt for him.

So maybe she should be crying because she was a fool who stupidly believed she could be enough for someone like him. Wouldn't it have been better if she had never gotten her hopes up? Whoever said "It's better to have loved and lost than never to have loved at all" was full of it. This wasn't better. This was worse. So much worse.

And it was going to be a long time before she felt like anything would ever be okay again.

***

"Dude, what the hell?"

Yeah, Sam was braced for this kind of reaction from Mason but was kind of hoping he'd be wrong. It had been twenty-four hours since he ended things with Shelby and started to put things in motion to leave town.

"Are you out of your freaking mind?" Mason

demanded. "What the hell am I supposed to do with this mess?"

"It's not a mess, Mason," Sam explained calmly. "It's a business. A lucrative business. You don't have to do a damn thing if you don't want to. I have a great crew who can run everything and all you'd have to do is collect money at the end of the month or you can sell it and use the money to get the hell out from under your parents' thumb."

The fierce look on his cousin's face told him he had maybe gone a little far.

"Look, all I'm saying is that you can use the money," Sam went on. "Do with it whatever you want."

"So why aren't you doing that? Did you suddenly win the lottery or something?"

He gave Mason a dry look. "We both know why I'm doing this."

"And I think you're a jackass for it. You're overreacting, Sam, and you're making a rash decision here. Why don't you take a few days and think about it?"

They were sitting out on the pier behind their great-grandfather's house and Sam had chosen this spot because there wouldn't be an audience. Turning his head, he looked at Mason. "A few days isn't going to make a difference. I'm not going to suddenly become the most respectable guy in town and, last I checked, I didn't have the ability to erase people's memories so...what's the point in sticking around?"

"Because you're going to regret it," Mason stated. "You know the minute you cross the bridge and get on the highway, you're going to regret it."

Part of him agreed but there was no way he was going to admit that out loud. "I disagree."

They sat in silence and Mason reached into the cooler that sat between them, pulled out a beer and handed it to

Sam before snagging one for himself. "Did you talk to your mom? Mallory?"

He nodded. "I talked to Mal about it yesterday and sat down with my mom this morning. She's been so busy with stuff around here or out with Colton and I hated to bog her down with my shit." He rolled his eyes. "She really does have a healthier love life than I do and I hate to admit it, but it's kind of hard to be around."

Beside him, Mason snickered. "I'll bet."

"The thing is, she said all the things you're saying which are the same things Mallory said. I appreciate everyone's concern, but this is something I have to do."

"Why?" Mason asked. "Just...why? The business is going strong. I get what happened with Shelby's folks sucked, but don't let it run you out of town!"

His shoulders sagged and he took a pull of his beer. Staring out at the Sound he said, "I can't be here and not be with her. It would be too hard." He shook his head. "I don't want to cause any problems for her and the only way I can guarantee that is by not being here."

Mason stared at him long and hard for several minutes. "She means a lot to you, doesn't she?"

He nodded. "She means everything."

"All the more reason not to leave, dude!" Mason yelled. "You're smarter than this!"

"You don't get it. You've never had this problem. You're the most eligible bachelor in Magnolia. Parents are practically throwing their daughters at you!"

"It's not as enticing as it sounds. It's exhausting and a little humiliating because no one is seeing who I really am. They're looking at my name and who my folks are. No one gives a damn about what I like or what I'm interested in. All they want is...hell, I don't even know."

"Shelby's folks want her with someone like you – a guy who's respectable and a stand-up guy with good manners or whatever." Then he glared at his cousin. "Funny how you were with me during most of my antics in this town and the only one everyone seems to remember is me."

Mason looked away guiltily.

"I don't blame you, Mason," Sam said solemnly. "I think it sucks but I know it's not your fault."

"Doesn't make me feel any better," Mason replied quietly. "You're practically getting run out of town for things we both did."

"I never should have come back. I should have given up the inheritance and just...gone back to Virginia. Then I never would have met Shelby and caused her so many problems or gotten myself excited about all the possibilities with the business. It's...it's just a shitty situation and I hate how I screwed up so many people's lives."

"Sam!" They both turned their heads toward the house where Susannah was standing out on the deck. "There's someone here to see you!" she called out.

His stomach sank and he prayed it wasn't Shelby coming here to try to talk to him. He wasn't sure he'd be able to take it. Slowly he rose to his feet and began to walk up the pier when he spotted a woman walking down the steps toward him. He froze when he realized who it was.

Laney.

*Shit.*

She was the last person he ever expected to show up looking for him, but as she stormed down the stairs, he had a feeling he knew exactly why she was here.

When she was standing directly in front of him, he braced himself for the verbal attack. She stood almost a foot shorter than him but right now, she looked pretty fierce.

"Hey, Laney," he forced himself to say.

"I just wanted you to know," she began calmly, "that you hurt the most amazing person in the world."

*Tell me something I don't know...*

"But I understand why you did it."

Say what?

"For what it's worth, I think her parents are wrong about pretty much everything. I think they treat Shelby like a child and don't approve of most of the things she does. Growing up as the pastor's kid, she was always under the microscope. And for all the years that I've known her, she never broke the rules." She paused. "Until you."

"Yeah and look where that got her," he murmured.

"It made her happier than I've ever seen her," Laney countered. "I've seen her blossom in a way I never thought I'd see. She was smiling and confident and finally coming out of her shell and believing in herself."

He really didn't want to hear this...

"You were good for her, Sam, but then you went and destroyed her." She glared at him and let that sink in. "I just left her house and I've never seen her like that. She didn't come to work today and I don't think she'll be in tomorrow."

"It's for the best, Laney. Believe it or not, I'm doing this *for* Shelby."

"You keep telling yourself that," she spat. "But let me leave you with this – she'll get over this. Eventually. She'll move on and her parents will introduce her to another boring jerk who she has no interest in and she'll go out with him and maybe even marry him because she'll feel like she has to. Like she owes them. But she'll never love him. Not like she loves you."

Damn.

"So while you move on and get to have your life, I hope

you remember the life you ruined here – not by staying, but by leaving. Think about that." And then she spun on her heel and stormed back the way she came.

Mason came up behind him and clapped a hand on Sam's shoulder. "Well, she certainly put you in your place."

"Shut up."

Stepping around him until they were facing each other, Mason said, "She's right, Sam. You can say all you want that you're doing this for her, but you never even talked to her or gave her a chance. You're being noble and I think that can be a good thing, but not in this particular situation."

It was all too much for him to think about – too much to take in. Most of the time when he was faced with making a decision, he made the wrong one. Was he doing that again?

No. All the other times he had been selfish and did what he wanted without taking anyone's feelings into consideration. This time he was only thinking of someone else – Shelby. She deserved to have the family relationship she always had without him messing it up.

Decision made – again – he forced himself to smile at his cousin. "I need to go up and do some packing."

Letting out a long and loud breath, Mason shook his head. "When are you planning on leaving?"

"Tomorrow. We're going to have a family dinner tonight with my mom, Mallory, Jake, and Colton."

He chuckled. "Wow. Even the boyfriend is coming. Nice."

Sam couldn't help but laugh. "Yeah. Even the boyfriend is coming. I think he's going to be around for a while."

"Good for them. Seriously, your mom deserves to be happy." He paused. "And so do you." He clapped his shoulder again. "Call me when you get settled back in

Virginia. Maybe I'll come up for a weekend and we can hang out."

"Sounds good." He stood back and watched his cousin leave but didn't follow to go back inside. He needed a little more time outside with nothing but the sounds of nature around him to help him get his head together.

Slowly, he walked back down the pier and resumed his spot at the end next to the cooler. Not that he wanted another beer, but...looking over his shoulder he looked over at the boathouse and stood up. The party deck was way more comfortable. Maybe a little time up there like he'd spent with Mallory would be better.

Or maybe going to Shelby's and telling her he was sorry and made a big mistake would be even better.

Yeah, no matter how confident he tried to sound in his decision to others, the thought of leaving was killing him.

*For her. You're doing this for her.*

His heart actually ached at the thought of leaving her and never seeing her again. Everyone assumed he was being selfish by leaving – including Shelby. That was fine. It was no different than what they had always thought of him. But he knew better. He knew exactly why he had to do this.

And maybe someday, Shelby would think about him and remember all of the great times they'd had together – all the laughing and great conversations, the way they had made love.

And hopefully someday...she'd forgive him.

## 13

THERE WAS a time when Shelby would simply resign herself to the way her life was going.

That time was over.

Looking around her house, she felt a sense of pride. She had done this – she had worked hard and saved her money and bought this little house all on her own. But as much as she loved it and loved all that it represented and all she had made it into, it wasn't her forever home.

At least, not without Sam here with her.

Never before had she felt the need to argue or fight so hard for something – had never felt so passionately about something – as she felt about their relationship. Maybe he didn't love her the way she loved him. Maybe this was all one-sided, but she wasn't going to know if she didn't ask! When he came over and told her it was over, she was too stunned to think clearly. Well, after sitting here and doing nothing but think, she now knew what she wanted to say. And if Sam still wanted to leave after it was all said and done, she would accept it and move on.

Eventually.

But she certainly wasn't going down without a fight.

With her inner pep talk complete, she picked up the bags she had by the front door and walked out. In her car, she kept reminding herself to be strong and not to back down. Sam might think he could talk over her or that she maybe didn't know what she was talking about, but boy was she ready to prove him – and everyone else – wrong.

Pulling into the long gravel drive that led to his family home, she was relieved to see that his truck was still there. Parking beside it, she let out a long breath and hoped the butterflies in her stomach would disappear after she got a few words out. Climbing from the car, she walked up the front steps and didn't hesitate to knock on the door.

"Shelby!" Susannah said with a warm smile. "What a wonderful surprise!"

And damn, she really did like Susannah but if she was going to keep up this momentum and confront Sam, she needed no distractions. "Hey, Susannah. Is Sam around?"

Her smile fell a little and she said, "He's down by the boathouse. You can come through the house or there's a path around the side..."

"I'll take the path, thank you," she said quickly and turned to go. Maybe it was a little rude, but it was now or never, and she was a woman on a mission. Walking around the house she admired all of the beautiful flowers and shrubs and gardens and knew Sam had played a large role in placing them there. She remembered the destruction from the storm and even a few weeks ago when she was here with him so much of this hadn't been here.

At the back of the house she spotted the pier and saw Sam standing on the deck of the boathouse. He looked so sad and alone and yet he took her breath away. Her first thought was to run to him – to run up those steps and spill her heart out to him. But a sense of calmness washed over her and she found her nerves settling down and she slowly made her way toward him – her footsteps soft enough that if he heard her, she couldn't tell.

When she was mere feet away, she cleared her throat to get his attention. The look he gave her broke her heart.

Defeated.

Weary.

"I have something to say to you, Sam," she stated boldly and was relieved when he didn't try to stop her. "Did it occur to you, even once, that maybe I disagree with my parents? Or how their opinion of what I choose to do with my life doesn't matter?"

"Shelby, we both know that's not the only issue here. It's the biggest one, but it's not the only one."

She took a few steps toward him. "I saw a side of my family that I'm not particularly proud of and you know what? It breaks my heart, but it doesn't mean they're right! If anything, what this entire situation did was open my eyes to all the ways they've been trying to control me and how little they think of me!"

"But it shouldn't be like that! I shouldn't have played a part in that!"

"You're not to blame here!" she cried. "They are! And... so am I! Don't you get it? If I had stood up to them sooner, we wouldn't be here fighting about this right now! I should have spoken up years ago about the way they were trying to dictate my life. You helped me see that, Sam, and it needed to happen." With as much bravery as she could muster, she reached out and grasped his hand in hers. "I'm thankful it happened."

If anything, his expression turned even bleaker. "I'm not going to break up your family, Shelby. Things will calm down and you'll talk things out and it will be better for all of you if I'm not here."

"No, it won't!" Tugging him closer, she looked up at him pleadingly. "You have no idea how happy I am that all this happened. My parents need a reality check and I think this was it! And I needed to stop being so damn wishy-washy where they're concerned. I need to live my life the way that I want to!"

"But...they're your family, Shelby..."

Releasing his hand, she reached up and cupped his face. "*We* can be a family, Sam. Me and you." Swallowing hard, she knew it was time for the big guns. Again. "I love you. I love you so damn much and I see a future for us. And it doesn't have to be here in Magnolia. If you really want to leave, I'll go with you! Just...give us a chance. Please." Tears stung her eyes. "It's okay if you don't love me – if you don't feel the same – just..."

She never got to finish because Sam's lips crashed down on hers as his arms tightly banded around her. It was wild and frantic and almost brutal, and yet nothing had ever felt sweeter. Shelby wanted to wrap herself around him and never let go. He maneuvered them over to one of the chaise lounges even as he continued to devour her.

Well...as they devoured each other.

When Sam lifted his head, she had no idea how much time had passed, but they were both breathing heavily. He rested his forehead against hers. "How can you even doubt that I love you?" he asked breathlessly. "From the moment I saw you that night, you were it for me."

"But..."

He shook his head. "No buts, Shelby. I felt like I had to leave because staying was hurting you and your family. I didn't want to be responsible for that. I thought leaving you would be best."

Shaking her head, she once again reached for his face, reveling in the feel of it. "That was never going to best for me. Ever. We are both guilty of not communicating with each other. I knew how you felt about being here in Magnolia and I knew how awkward things went with my folks, and rather than talking about it, I used sex as a distraction."

A lopsided grin was his first response. "Greatest distraction ever. Feel free to use that one again."

She laughed softly. "Deal."

His gaze raked over her. "I don't even know what to say. I can't believe you're really here."

"Why?"

"Because...I don't know...I guess I thought you'd agree with me and why I needed to leave."

Pushing him slightly off of her, she said, "No, you thought a girl like me wouldn't fight back. That's been my problem my entire life. I've never been bold enough to stand up for myself – until I met you."

His smile grew. "You're feeling all kinds of sassy right now, aren't you?"

Nodding, she said, "I really do. I kind of like this."

"You should." Leaning forward, he kissed her softly. "Thank you for being braver than I ever could be."

"Can I ask you something?"

"Anything."

"All your life, you've done what you wanted and didn't care what anyone else thought. Why now? Why does it bother you so much now?"

"Because it wasn't just me anymore. There was you and I hated hearing anyone say anything negative about you."

Smiling, she placed a soft kiss on his lips. "But even before me you were having issues with it. Why?"

"It's hard to move forward and make something of your life when people are so determined to keep reminding you of your mistakes. And for most of my life, I had Pops here to act as a buffer. With him gone, it was all on me to defend myself and it scared the hell out of me. Just like your father did at lunch, I get the comparisons and how I'm nothing like my great-grandfather, but..."

"Did he ever ask you to be like him?" she interrupted.

"What do you mean?"

"Your great-grandfather. Did he ever tell you that you had to be like him?"

Sam shook his head. "No. Pops never said I had to do anything, but he always encouraged me to do what I love and do it well." He let out a small laugh. "After I screwed up somewhere."

"You were a kid, Sam, and I think he knew that."

He shifted until he was stretched out beside her. "I know, but it bothers me more than you know that he'll never see me succeed. His last memory of me is being a screw-up."

"You have to stop saying that. If he truly believed that, he wouldn't have left you a business that meant so much to him."

Sitting up a little straighter, Sam stared down at her like her statement shocked him.

"Think about it – I don't believe Ezekiel left you the business because he was punishing you. I think he did it because he knew you were the perfect person to keep it going and make it grow."

He looked visibly shaken.

"Sam?"

"I...I never thought of it like that. I mean, he left Mallory the shop..."

"Because he knew she was the perfect person for it. She was passionate about it and would make sure it kept going here in the town he loved so much." Smiling, she caressed his cheek. "You've been looking at his gift the wrong way all this time."

He sagged down beside her. "Holy shit."

"I want you to know something," she said after a minute. "If you want to leave Magnolia and go back to Virginia, I meant what I said, I want to go with you."

"Shelby..."

"It's true!" she quickly interrupted. "I love this town and my job, but I love you more."

Placing a gentle kiss on the tip of her nose, he said, "You're amazing. I don't deserve you." One strong hand came up and mimicked her move, caressing her cheek. "I love you, Shelby Abbott. I love everything about you."

She wanted to weep with joy. "I never thought I'd hear you say that."

"It's true," he whispered. "I love you so much and I still can't believe you're mine."

Hugging him close, Shelby simply let herself enjoy the moment. She was his and he was hers and everything else would have to work itself out.

"There's just one thing," he began cautiously as he pulled back.

"What's that?"

"I can't ask you to come to Virginia with me. I just can't."

And just like that, her heart sank. Was all this for nothing? Was he still going to leave?

It took all of three seconds for Sam to realize his mistake. The shocked look on Shelby's face spoke volumes.

"What I mean is...I'm not going back to Virginia. This is where I want to be – here in Magnolia with you."

She visibly relaxed and let out a long breath. "Oh my goodness, you scared me there for a minute."

"Shelby Abbott, I want to be where you are. Where you sleep is where I plan to make my bed," he said softly.

She gave him a trembly smile as tears formed in her eyes. "That's the most beautiful thing I've ever heard."

"That's good, because you're the most beautiful woman I've ever seen."

Blushing, she said, "Sam, please...you don't have to say that."

He held her face firmly in his hand. "I know I don't have to say it, but it doesn't make it any less true. You, Shelby Abbott, are beautiful. And strong and talented and sweet and funny and...you're everything."

And the look of pure gratitude on her face told him everything he needed to know. Shelby wasn't used to people believing in her or praising her – something he planned on doing for her from this day forward.

Unable to help himself, he leaned in and kissed her again. A cool breeze blew around them and he wished they were someplace warm – and inside – so as much as he hated to have to stop kissing her, he knew they needed to move. Slowly he moved off the chaise and held out a hand to help her stand.

"I'm supposed to have dinner with my family tonight," he said, holding her close to shield her from the cold. "But now I want to go home with you and just ignore the rest of the world for a little while."

She smiled up at him. "How about you go have your dinner and come over later?"

That was completely unacceptable. Shaking his head, Sam countered, "How about you come to dinner with me and the family and then we go back to your place together for dessert?"

Her smile grew. "I don't want to impose…"

"Impose? Are you kidding me? I think someone may break out the champagne when we tell them I'm staying!" he said with a laugh. "C'mon, let's go inside and warm up and share the news."

Together they walked hand-in-hand down the stairs and up the pier where they ran into Mallory and Jake, who were also heading over to the house. Sam caught the knowing smile on his sister's face and simply shrugged as if to say, "You were right."

"Hey, you two!" Mallory said, putting her attention primarily on Shelby. "Are you joining us for dinner?"

Sam placed his arm around Shelby and kept her so close that he could see her blush.

"Um…Sam just invited me, but I feel bad because I didn't bring anything to contribute to the meal." She smiled up at him and then looked back at Mallory. "My mother always told me to make sure I brought dessert or a bottle of wine when I went to someone's house for dinner."

It was on the tip of Sam's tongue to remind her how her mother was a big fat hypocrite but opted to keep that to himself. Instead, he placed a kiss on the top of her head. "I think you're bringing something better than dessert or wine to dinner."

"Oh really?" Mallory said in a sing-song voice. "Do tell!"

"Sam..." Shelby said, clearly feeling a bit embarrassed.

"You'll have to wait and find out when we're all up at the house. Mom's going to want to hear this too."

"Come on!" Mallory whined even as she laughed. "You have to tell me!"

"We'll be in the house in three minutes, Mal," Sam said with a laugh of his own. "Don't be such a baby."

"You...don't be such a baby," Mallory countered.

"Mal," Jake interrupted. "Give your brother a break."

"Thank you," Sam said over his shoulder.

"Fine. Don't tell me," Mallory said and then she gave a giddy little hop. "Oh! I forgot to tell you! I finally decided on a new name for the shop!"

"Finally," Jake said, laughing.

"And?" Sam asked. "What's it gonna be?"

"Shore Décor!" she exclaimed. "Isn't it perfect!"

"I like it!" Sam agreed. "Good job, Mal!"

"I love it!" Shelby chimed in. "It's the perfect name for the shop."

As they walked up to the deck, Sam spotted his mother looking at all of them through the kitchen window with a big smile on her face. He had to admit, part of him felt a little foolish for having to admit he was staying after making such a big deal about leaving.

Which reminded him – he needed to call Mason as soon as he could to tell him there was a change of plans.

Susannah slid open the back door and looked at him expectantly. He knew he couldn't keep her waiting.

"I'm staying in Magnolia," he announced and was immediately embraced from every side. His mother was hugging him, his sister was hugging him, Jake was patting him on the back, and he still managed to keep Shelby close. "I know I said I was leaving, but..."

"Who cares!" Mallory said excitedly. "You're staying! You're really staying!"

He nodded and was thankful when he was released. Colton came out and shook his hand and it wasn't nearly as awkward as he thought it would be. "You've made your mom and all of us very happy, Sam," he said.

"Thanks, Colt." Yeah, it looked like he was going to have to acknowledge the fact that Colton was going to be part of the family.

"Come on," Susannah said, ushering everyone into the kitchen. "Dinner's almost ready."

"I hope I'm not intruding," Shelby began, but just as he suspected, his mother waved her off.

"Nonsense. You're always welcome here," Susannah reassured as she fluttered around the kitchen getting another place setting.

He kissed Shelby on the cheek. "Can you grab me something to drink? I just want to shoot Mason a text and let him know the news." As she walked away, Sam pulled his phone from his pocket and quickly pulled up his cousin's contact info.

**Good news. You're no longer the owner of a landscaping company.**

He hit send and couldn't help but wish that he could see the look on Mason's face as he read the message.

**What if I said I didn't want to give it back?**

Chuckling, Sam knew Mason was kidding with him, but still...he felt like he needed to put him in his place.

**Then I'd have to make sure I helped your parents find the next great girl for you and**

**promise to make sure I'd convince you to settle down.**

They both knew it was a lie, but it still made him laugh just thinking about it.

**Fine. You can have it back plus an extra hundred bucks just...keep all your happy relationship news to yourself. If my folks get wind of it, they'll be impossible to live with.**

Interesting.

**How do you know I have happy relationship news?**

Three dots instantly appeared as Mason was already responding.

**Please. There's only one reason for you to stay. And BTW, I'm glad you pulled your head out of your ass.**

Shelby stepped up beside him with a glass of sweet tea for him.

**Me too. TTYL**

Sliding the phone back into his pocket, he took the glass from Shelby's hand. "Thanks, baby," he said.

Susannah called them all to the table and over the next two hours they talked about the progress on the bed and breakfast, the expansion Mallory wanted to do to the shop, and the plans Sam had for his business now that he was officially staying. They were getting ready to head into the spring season and most of what he was doing now was still a lot of cleanup from the hurricane and general, routine landscape jobs. Once the warmer weather returned, he hoped to have several commercial contracts outside of the Magnolia Sound area so he could branch out a bit.

"That's ambitious," Jake said. "We should talk about

teaming up on new construction projects I'm working on. It would be nice to have an in-house landscape designer we could offer to clients."

Sam nodded. "That sounds great. We should set up a time to talk about it."

"Sam, why don't you and Shelby come for dinner one night next week?" Mallory suggested. "You and Jake could talk shop and Shelby and I can get to know each other a little more."

Sam looked at Shelby and was happy to see she was smiling and in total agreement. "That sounds great!"

By the time they had finished with dessert, Sam was more than ready to leave. They all said their goodbyes and when they were out on the driveway and next to Shelby's car, he pulled her in close and kissed her.

"Thank you," he murmured against her lips.

"Mmm...for what?"

"For coming here tonight."

She was looking pretty pleased with herself as she smiled up at him. "Well, one of us had to be the voice of reason."

Laughing, he said, "Absolutely and I'm so glad you were the one to realize that." He looked over her shoulder and saw two suitcases in her back seat. "Hey, what's up with those?"

Moving out of his arms, she saw where he was looking and started to laugh.

"What? What's so funny?"

Opening the car door, she pointed to the luggage. "Well, this one right here has all of your clothes you left at my house."

"What?!" he cried incredulously. "I thought I took everything!"

"They were in the laundry. They're wrinkly, but they're clean."

"Oh." He paused and then frowned. "Wait, why did you pack them up?"

"What if I came here and couldn't convince you to give us another chance? I wouldn't want your stuff to stay at my house," she reasoned. "You would want and need it back, so I was simply bringing it to you."

Okay, he could see her logic, but...

"And what's in the other one?"

Her smile turned a little impish. "That one has a bunch of stuff for me."

Confused, he asked, "What for?"

"That was in case you *did* want to give us another chance but still wanted to go back to Virginia. It was so I could leave with you tonight if you wanted."

And he had never been so humbled in all his life. This girl – this amazingly incredible girl – was far braver and more confident and hell...smarter than he could ever be. Tugging her in close, he kissed her soundly before saying, "Let's go home."

She laughed softly against his lips. "I thought you'd never ask."

# EPILOGUE

## SIX WEEKS LATER...

"Did you pick up something for dessert?"

"No."

"How come?"

"Because my mother always brings something for dessert. It's kind of her thing."

Sam nodded as he placed the pitcher of sweet tea on the table. Behind him, Shelby was moving around the kitchen putting the finishing touches on the meal. It was the first time they were having her parents over for dinner – or even seeing them – since that fateful day at the church. If it were up to him, he would have put this off for a little longer, but he knew there wasn't a reason for it. They had nothing to hide and nothing to be ashamed of so...if Steve and Caroline Abbott had a problem with them, it was on them and no one else.

"Are you sure you don't want a buffer here?" he asked. "My mom and Colton or even Jake and Mallory could be here in fifteen minutes or less."

She laughed softly. "No they couldn't. It's not like they're just sitting at home waiting for our call."

"Well...they kind of are."

"Sam!"

"What? We both know this has the potential to go horribly wrong. I wanted to make sure we had a backup plan if we needed them." He paused. "Actually, I asked Mason too, but he was heading out of town for some wedding. One of his college buddies is getting married; otherwise he'd be here because he said he wanted a front-row seat to this dinner."

She studied him for a moment before she started to laugh.

"What? What's so funny?"

"Laney's waiting at home too, just in case I need her."

Sweeping her up into his arms he kissed her. "Look at you being all devious. I think I really am a bad influence on you," he teased, but she swatted him away as soon as she was back on her feet.

"Believe it or not, I've always been devious. I just hide it fairly well."

"Baby, you hide it really well. And besides, you're far too sweet to be devious."

She gave him a sassy look. "I think you're forgetting all that I've accomplished in the last several weeks." Crossing her arms, she leaned against the kitchen counter. "I went and hunted you down and convinced you that you loved me."

"Well...you didn't really have to convince me..."

"I packed up my belongings and was ready to move to Virginia with you."

"You had one suitcase..."

"I put both my parents in their place and got them to apologize to us," she said smugly.

"Okay, that one was impressive."

"And...let's not forget yesterday's accomplishment..."

Yeah, yesterday had been a bit surreal and as much as he had wanted to decline the offer, he couldn't.

"Go ahead," he said dramatically. "Finish gloating."

"I managed to get you to be the landscape designer for the Ezekiel Coleman Memorial Park," she said, her tone going soft and sweet. "Located right behind the First Baptist Church of Magnolia Sound."

Sam had sworn to himself he wouldn't do any work for her father on the church park, but when Steve called and told him about the idea Shelby proposed and the money that had been raised for the project, he couldn't turn it down. Not only was it bridging the gap between Shelby, him, and her parents, it was going to be a labor of love for his great-grandfather. How could he turn that down?

Stepping in close, he braced his hands on either side of her, effectively caging her in. "You, Shelby Abbott, are a force to be reckoned with."

That statement seemed to please her immensely.

"I bet you never thought a girl like me could do so much, huh?"

Moving in close until they were touching from head to toe, he said, "A girl *like* you? No. But the girl you are? Hell yes. I knew you were someone amazing all along and I'm glad you're finally realizing that about yourself."

"That's all thanks to you," she said softly, going up on her tiptoes to kiss him.

He was wrapped around her and ready to really sink into the kiss when the doorbell rang. Sam muttered a curse even as Shelby began to laugh. She stepped out of his arms and held her hand out to him. "Ready?"

"As long as you're by my side, I think I can take on anything."

# A SNEAK PEEK

## IN CASE YOU DIDN'T KNOW

(Coming July 23rd, 2019)

"Success." Mason Bishop looked around the room with a satisfied grin. Sure he was alone and talking to himself, but he was alone in a place of his own and it was beyond exciting. It was something he should have done long ago, but he'd let himself be guilted long enough.

Collapsing down on his new sectional, he studied his surroundings with a sense of accomplishment. It was something he was always going to do, but a week ago he had hit his limit at home and decided the time had finally come.

Of course the fact that his cousin Sam kept poking at him because he still lived with his parents had helped, but...

As if on cue, his phone rang and there was Sam's name on the screen.

"Hey!"

"So?" Sam asked giddily. "Is it glorious? Please tell me it's glorious!"

Mason couldn't help but laugh. "I just put the last of the

boxes in the trash so I haven't had the time for it to feel particularly glorious yet, but..."

"Okay, fine. Pretend, for crying out loud. You're in your own place and it's filled with your own stuff. Doesn't it feel great?"

It would be fun to keep needling one another, but to what end? "You know what? It does," he said with a big grin. "I slept here last night but there were boxes and crap everywhere. Now everything is put away and...yeah, I guess it is kind of glorious."

"There you go! Now don't you feel like a complete idiot for waiting for so long?"

"Weren't you living with your mom up until a couple of months ago?"

"Dude, that was totally different. I'd been living on my own up in Virginia for years. It was only when I was forced to move here that I *chose* to live with my mother. Apples and oranges."

"Maybe."

"No maybes about it," Sam countered. "And now Shelby and I are living together and it's awesome."

"You sure that's a good idea? Moving in together so soon? Her father's a pastor. The gossip mill must be going crazy with the news!"

"Thanks. Like I needed the reminder," Sam deadpanned.

"And?"

"And what?"

"C'mon, are you telling me there's been no backlash? No one spouting how you're living in sin and whatnot?"

Sam let out a low laugh. "Oh, they spout it all the time, but we're good with it. We both know this is it for us and if anyone really starting hassling us, we're more than okay with going to the courthouse, making it legal, and shutting everyone up."

Mason was pretty sure his jaw hit the floor. "Wait... what? Are you serious? Making it...? Who are you and what have you done with my cousin!"

That just made Sam laugh harder. "When you know, you know. And with Shelby...I know."

And damn if he couldn't hear his cousin's smile.

It was enough to make a guy sick.

"Wow...just..." He let out a long breath. "I never thought I'd live to see the day."

"Yeah, well...me either. But like I said, she's it for me. But I appreciate the uh...concern." He laughed again. "That's what that was, right? You being concerned?"

"Um...yeah. Sure. We can call it that," Mason said with a snicker. "We're family and we just look out for one another, right?"

"Yes, we do. But enough about me. Weren't we talking about you and the decisions you're making for your own life?" He paused. "You know I was seriously just thinking of your own sanity, Mason. Every day I watched you die a little more while under your parents' thumbs."

"I know and now that it's done, I can't believe I didn't do it sooner–like as soon as I graduated college."

"Hell, I'm still surprised you opted to move back here at all."

Raking a hand through his hair, he looked up at the ceiling. "I tossed around the idea of moving somewhere else, but...believe it or not, I like it here. I see all the things I want to do and help change. And if it means I have to live under the watchful eye of my folks, I'll live."

"They'll get hobbies eventually, right?" Sam teased.

"God I hope so."

"They will. And either way, this move is going to be great for you. Trust me."

He didn't need his cousin to tell him that, he already knew it.

Could feel it too.

Last night when he'd carried in the last box and closed the door behind him, Mason felt like he had taken his first free breath.

Sad, right?

"I do trust you and I know the time was right because everything fell into place. The house - even though it's only a rental - is the perfect size for me. A couple of years from now I might be ready to buy a place, but for now this works."

"If you'd make a damn decision on the bar Pops left you, you know you could have afforded something of your own. I mean, why are you holding on to this place? Let it go already!"

Yeah, everyone had been in his face about the Mystic Magnolia and Mason had to admit, the whole thing still stumped him. Everyone else got an inheritance that made sense except him. Granted, he never felt the closeness to Pops his sisters or his cousins did, but to be left a decrepit old dive bar just seemed like a slap in the face.

Although–if he was being honest–he'd admit there was one *tiny* reason he was still holding on to it...

"I'll deal with it when I'm ready," he stated, unwilling to let his mind wander any more than it already had. "The lawyer said there wasn't a rush and everything is being handled - bills are being paid and all so...I'm still trying to wrap my brain around it all."

"You mean why Pops gave you the place only old locals

go to?" Sam teased. "And I mean *old*! No one under the age of sixty-five goes there!"

"Okay, that's not *that* old…"

"C'mon, fess up. Pops took you there when you were younger, didn't he," Sam prodded. "The place must hold some significance to you and that's why he felt like you should be the one to have it."

"Why would I go to a bar with my great-grandfather? That's just…it's weird, Sam."

"Some could say it was like bonding, but whatever."

"Look, Pops never took me to the Mystic Magnolia or any other bar so…I'm stumped."

"Did he give you a letter? I thought we all got letters."

Rubbing a hand over his face, Mason let out a long breath. "He said a lot of things in my letter but none explained why he thought I should get that place."

"Really? Huh…that's strange. What did he say?"

"It was like he was channeling his inner Yoda or something. He spoke in all kinds of riddles. It was weird."

"Like what?"

Ugh…this really wasn't something he wanted to talk about right now. He was feeling all good and proud of himself and had been ready to order a pizza and kick back and enjoy it here in his new place and now his cousin was crapping all over his good mood.

"Look, you um…you wanna come over for some pizza?" he said, hoping to change the subject. "I was just getting ready to order one when you called."

Luckily Sam could be easily distracted.

"Wish I could, but rain check, okay? Shelby and I have dinner plans with Jake and Mallory. You wanna join us?"

The laugh escaped before he could stop it. "Right. Why

wouldn't I want to be the fifth wheel at dinner? I think I'll pass."

Catching his meaning, Sam laughed. "Yeah. Okay, I get it. Are you going to the benefit concert tomorrow night?"

"Shit," he murmured. "Is that tomorrow?"

Sam chuckled. "Yup. I think your mom bought out the entire VIP section."

He groaned. "Of course she did." He paused. "Wait, the Magnolia Amphitheater has a VIP section? Seriously?"

"Sure. Most places do."

"Still, that place isn't all that big–like 2,500 seats max."

"And that has to do with VIP seats...why?"

He groaned again. "Never mind. It doesn't really matter. We'll all be there so...wait, who's playing?"

"A couple of bands, I think. I didn't pay much attention either, but they're all somewhat local."

For the life of him, the name of the band escaped him, but it didn't really matter. "Go have dinner and tell everyone I said hey and I'll see you all at the show tomorrow."

"Yeah, sure. Sounds like a plan. Have a good night."

"You too."

After he hung up, Mason stretched his arms out along the top of the sofa cushions and smiled. He could order some pizza and maybe invite some friends over and not have to hear about what other people his age were doing or who had just gotten married or engaged or who would be a suitable spouse for him. Seriously, he loved his parents but their obsession with his life had gotten out of control.

Ten days ago had been the breaking point.

He had come home from work to find his mother having wine with a woman he'd never met before. Leslie....something. Mason had figured she was involved in one of his mother's many charity projects and said a brief hello and went to go change so he could go for a run.

That's when it all went wrong.

"Mason, sweetie," his mother said in her best southern drawl. "You can't go for a run. You have dinner reservations in thirty minutes with Leslie."

The rage he had felt in that moment had been like nothing he'd ever felt before. In the past he'd dealt with being introduced to women his parents thought would be a good match for him or being asked to take out one of their friends' daughters, but this was the first time he had been so blatantly ambushed in his own home.

Forcing a smile onto his face, he looked at Leslie and said, "I'm so sorry you were misled, but...I already have plans this evening." When he turned to leave the room, his mother had jumped to her feet and come after him, berating him for being rude.

"Rude?" he snapped. "You made dinner reservations for me with a stranger without talking to me about it and *I'm* being rude? This is it! I'm not doing this anymore! You have interfered with my life for the last time!"

The argument had gone on for hours and even though his father had come home and tried to calm things down, it was too late. The damage was done. Mason had walked to his room, packed a bag and walked out.

And hadn't talked to either parent since.

He spent a week staying at Magnolia on the Beach - a small local hotel - and frantically combed the real estate ads looking for a place to live. The house was a complete godsend and when it was available immediately, he knew it was meant to be his. Furnishing it had been a breeze since his cousin Mallory owned the local decor place in town and helped him and then his sisters had both taken turns bringing some of his things from home over to him. They could be total pains in the ass at times, but he was thankful for them right now.

It was quiet and for a long minute he sat there and enjoyed it and then...not so much. He wasn't used to it and he had a feeling it would be a while before he was. Suddenly the thought of sitting home eating pizza wasn't quite so appealing, but then again, neither was going out to a bar or going out to eat alone.

Maybe he should've been the fifth wheel.

"This is ridiculous," he murmured coming to his feet. He'd lived in this town his entire life. Surely he could go out and grab something to eat and maybe run into a friend or two and kill some time before coming back here alone.

Or maybe...not alone.

Hell, he could finally bring a woman home instead of either going to her place or going to a motel!

The idea had merit.

But then...it didn't.

Honestly, he was tired, sweaty, and hungry. There was no shame in admitting that a quiet night in his own home was really what he wanted. Still, now he didn't want pizza, he wanted something with a little more substance. Feeling like he had a bit of a plan, he walked with purpose into his new en suite bathroom to shower so he could go out and grab something to eat before settling in for the night with some Netflix.

---

"I think my virginity is growing back."

"Engine grease under your fingernails isn't very attractive, Scar. Maybe that's why guys aren't banging down your door to ask you out. But that's just my opinion."

Scarlett Jones looked down at her hands and frowned.

Damn.

With a shrug, she walked back into her bathroom to rewash her hands. Yeah, she wasn't a girly girl. She grew up working in her father's garage alongside him and her three brothers and it turned out she really had a gift for working on motorcycles. If the engine grease and the smell of gasoline on her didn't turn guys off, the fact that she was fiercely independent did.

Did it bother her? Yes.

Enough to make her quit? No.

Glancing up at her reflection, Scarlett couldn't help but wonder what was wrong with her. In just about every other aspect of her life, she was confident—sometimes overly so. She was smart and caring and always willing to help out anyone in need. Everyone was always saying how great she was.

And yet, she hadn't been in a relationship in a long time.

Like...a really long time.

Hence the fear of her virginity growing back.

Turning off the water, she shook out her hands as she continued to stare at herself. While there wasn't anything particularly remarkable about her, she was bold enough to know she was attractive—long, wavy brown hair, dark brown eyes, and -if she did say so herself, a pretty kickass body. So why couldn't she seem to attract a decent guy?

"You're not pissed at me, are you?"

Reaching for a hand towel, Scarlett pulled herself from her thoughts and looked over at her best friend Courtney. With a smile, she replied, "Nah. That would be a pretty stupid reason to be mad. I had grease under my nails and you were just pointing it out. No biggie."

Only...it did bother her.

Not that Courtney had pointed it out, but that it was there in the first place and she hadn't noticed it.

And it probably wasn't the first time.

"Are you sure? Because you just sort of up and walked away."

Scarlett tossed the towel aside before holding up her hands and wiggling her fingers. "To get rid of the grease!" With a small laugh, she walked past Courtney and back out into her bedroom. "Okay, where are we going tonight? Do I need to change?"

Looking down at herself, she seriously hoped not. She was comfortable. For the most part, they stuck to the local pubs and going out in jeans and a nice top were fine. But lately, Courtney had been wanting to broaden their horizons and that meant dressing up more.

She bit her tongue to prevent her from complaining out loud.

Courtney walked across the room and flopped down on the bed with a dramatic sigh.

*That can't be good*, Scarlett thought, but waited her friend out.

Busying herself with straightening up her room and not looking for something else to wear, she mentally prayed Courtney would just say what was on her mind.

"I think I want to move," she finally said and Scarlett immediately gasped in shock.

"What? Why? Where?"

Sitting up, Courtney flipped her hair over her shoulder and sighed again. "Anywhere. I'm just never going to do anything or meet anyone if I stay here. I'm over small-town life."

They'd had this conversation multiple times and for the most part, Scarlett was used to it. Walking over, she sat down on the bed beside her. "Okay, what brought this on? Last weekend we went out and had a great time and I seem to remember seeing you make out with Mike Ryan." Then she winked. "And I distinctly remember watching you wave goodbye to me as you left with him."

Courtney fell back on the bed. "Yeah, and it was good and the sex was good, but...it's like it's always the same guys! We've been hanging out with the same people we've known since elementary school!"

"That's not true. We're heading into the peak tourist season! You know it's going to be crazy around here for the next six weeks or so. Maybe you'll meet someone..."

"You don't get it, Scar. I don't want to be the girl the tourists hook up with for a quick weekend fling or the girl the locals pass the time with until they can hit on the tourists! I'm just...I'm ready for a change!"

"Okay, okay," she soothed, falling back next to Courtney. "How about this...let's just go out tonight and grab something to eat and then we'll pick up some ice cream on the way home and just have a mellow night? How does that sound?"

"Boring," Courtney said with a pout. "And the exact reason why I'm done with small town life."

"Hey! I'm kind of taking offense to that! I know I'm not the most exciting person in the world, but..." Sitting up, Scarlett immediately bounced off the bed.

"You're right, you're right, you're right," Courtney said, standing up. "That was uncalled for." She gave Scarlett a long hug before pulling back. "I'm just in a funk and I'm bored and...don't listen to me. I'll get over it."

And the thing was, Scarlett knew she would, but it didn't mean she could just ignore the situation either.

"Look," she began cautiously, "I'm bored too. It's not like a whole lot of exciting stuff happens around here or that I've got all kinds of interesting things going on..."

"Now that's not true. You could be doing so much more if you would just share your hobby with..."

"Lalalalala!" Scarlett cried out before stopping to glare at her friend. "I swore you to secrecy and you promised to never bring it up!"

Courtney looked around the room in confusion. "Who's going to hear me? It's just the two of us!"

There was a slight chance she was being paranoid, but there was no way she was going to tell anyone other than Courtney what she'd been doing in her spare time.

"Fine. Whatever," she murmured. "Can we go grab something to eat now? I'm starving."

And yeah, there was a little snap in her voice that she was regretting.

They walked out of the bedroom and Scarlett picked up her purse and keys and followed Courtney out the door.

"So not the fun night I was hoping for," she said under her breath. At her car, she paused and apologized. "I'm sorry I snapped at you. That was wrong of me."

Courtney—ever the drama queen—merely shrugged.

Awesome.

"You want to go to Café Magnolia or The Sand Bar for burgers?"

"Ugh...I know their burgers are legendary, but why won't they change the name of the damn place! It's not very appetizing to go and eat someplace that has the word sand in their title."

"So you want to go to the café?"

"I didn't say that," Courtney was quick to amend. "I mean, we both know a girls night requires burgers."

"And fries," Scarlett said with a grin as they climbed into her car.

The Sand Bar was like most of the businesses in Magnolia Sound–an institution. It had been around for at least twenty years and was in need of a renovation, but business was too good to close down and get it done. When the hurricane hit a little more than six months ago, it seemed like the logical time to finally freshen the place up. Unfortunately, old Mr. Hawkins simply fixed the roof and replaced a couple of windows and declared The Sand Bar open once again for business a week after Hurricane Amelia blew through.

"I'm getting the bacon cheeseburger, fries, and possibly onion rings," Courtney declared as they drove along Main Street. Turning her head, she grinned at Scarlett. "And I think you should share an order of fried pickles with me."

Her stomach hurt just thinking about all the food, but she kept that to herself. Fried pickles definitely weren't her thing, but she'd eat a couple and move on. "Sure. Why not?"

The parking lot was crowded, but that wasn't anything new. The location was prime–on the beach side of the street–and there was indoor and outdoor seating, live entertainment, and a full bar. Honestly, Scarlett never cared much for coming here to drink, she was all about the food. Once she was parked and they were making their way toward the front entrance, the smell of food had her stomach growling.

Loudly.

"Totally not lady-like, Scar," Courtney teased even as she worked her way through the crowd and managed to find them a small booth in the corner.

"How do you do that?"

"Do what?"

"Always find us a place to sit?"

"It's my lone super-power," she said dryly as she flagged a waiter over. Once their orders were placed, Courtney began scanning the room. "I swear, even the tourists are the same ones."

Scarlett looked around and frowned. "Seriously? How can you tell?"

"Because we've been doing this for what feels like forever. Maybe they'll be some different faces at the concert tomorrow. You're still coming with me, right?"

Their server came back and placed their drinks down and Scarlett eagerly reached for hers. There was no way she could admit she wasn't looking forward to the concert, but she still needed a little sweet tea to bide her time.

"Nice delay tactic." Courtney knew her too well. With a weary sigh, she asked, "Tell me why you don't want to go."

"I don't know, Court. The amphitheater is small and the crowds are going to be crazy! We're going to be up in the nosebleed section and packed in like sardines! And on top of that, it's going to be ninety degrees out! Call me crazy, but that is not my idea of a good time."

"Why are you like this?" Courtney whined. "It's like you just refuse to have fun!"

"That's ridiculous! I have fun all the time! I just don't find it enjoyable to stand around and sweat when I don't have to!"

"You spend so much time working in your dad's garage

and it's always hot in there! Every time I've ever seen you there, you're sweating!"

"And that's because I have to be there!" she cried with more than a little frustration. "When I'm there, I'm working. I work, because I need money! And sometimes that means working in a building with little to no air conditioning!"

"Scarlett..."

"I'm forced to do it for work so why would I opt to do it on a night out when I'm supposed to be having fun?"

"Look, we both know you don't have to work at the garage, you choose to."

"I need the income..."

"Yeah, yeah, yeah...I get it. You use the second job to feed your hobby supplies," she said with a hint of sarcasm. "You work too much and you're always saving and you live frugally. It's admirable."

"But...?"

"But...you are way too uptight! No one is thinking about it being hot out, Scarlett! We're all like 'Yay! Concert!' Why can't you do the same?"

Seriously? "When have I ever simply followed the herd, Court? That's not me."

"Okay, fine. It's not, but...can't you just do it this once? C'mon! It's going to be so much fun! For one night can't you forget about your jobs and be a little carefree? You might actually enjoy it."

So many comments were on the tip of her tongue–most of them snarky–but Scarlett opted to keep them to herself. It was easy for people like Courtney to be carefree and not obsess about their finances. And while she didn't begrudge her friend having a family who always was and probably always would be financially stable, there was also no way for her to fully understand the anxiety that plagued her daily.

Growing up poor—and knowing that everyone you knew wasn't—wasn't something you got over. From the time Scarlett first started school, she knew she was different. Besides never having anything new for herself, she was dressed more like a boy than a girl. Looking back now she could almost laugh about it, but back then, it had been beyond painful. Her father had done the best he could and she loved him for it. She just wished someone had stepped in and tried to explain to Dominic Jones that raising a daughter was very different from raising sons. Her brothers were all fine—in their own annoying way. All three of them. But they were boys who had been raised by a strong male role model.

They'd also had more time with their mother before she died from colon cancer when Scarlett was only four. Kandace Jones had fought hard to win her battle with the deadly disease, but it was too much for her. There were days when her memories of her mother were so strong it was as if she were sitting right there with her, and other days it was like she couldn't remember a thing and would be devastated.

Either way, her father had struggled to raise four kids on his own and apparently it was easier to treat them all equally—like boys—rather than figuring out that Scarlett wanted nothing more than to be treated like a girl.

Something she still struggled with.

Maybe that was another reason why she couldn't seem to find anyone she was interested in dating. It was hard to find the balance between being the girly-girl she longed to be and the tough-as-nails mechanic she presented to the world.

A damn dilemma indeed.

Although if anyone dared to look in her closet who didn't know anything about her, they'd only see the girly stuff.

Way too much of it.

"Hey," Courtney said with a growing smile. "Just when you thought there were no new faces in the crowd..."

Scarlett turned her head and tried to see who her friend was talking about. "Who are you looking at?"

"I don't think I've seen him here before. I mean...I suppose it's possible, but I always heard he tended to hit bars and restaurants out of town–especially since we graduated."

Frowning, Scarlett continued to scan the crowd. "So it's someone we know?"

"Oh, good lord. I think he got even better looking..."

Now her curiosity was seriously piqued. Still, not one face in the crowd looked familiar and with a huff of frustration, she faced Courtney again. "Who the hell are you talking about?"

"Mason Bishop," she replied before taking a sip of her beer. "He's a little too pretty for my taste, but still, you have to appreciate a fine looking man." Putting her drink down, she looked at Scarlett. "What's with the face?"

Doing her best to put a relaxed smile on her face, she replied, "What do you mean?"

"You were practically scowling. Why?"

With a shrug, Scarlett reached for her own drink and wished it was alcohol. "I really wasn't."

"Yes, you were. Now spill it. What's up?"

If there was one thing Scarlett was certain of, it was that Courtney would continue to badger her until she told her what was up.

So she did.

"Guys like him? Like Mason? They're what's wrong with the world!"

Courtney's eyes went wide. "Um...what?"

Nodding, she looked over her shoulder and spotted him and glared briefly. When she turned back to Courtney, she explained. "Everything comes easy to guys like him. Like it's not enough that he comes from one of the founding families here in town, but his folks are wealthy and success-ful, his sisters are both super nice and pretty, and he looks like a damn model!"

"Scarlett..."

"No, I'm serious! Do you remember what he was like in school?"

"Uh...yeah..."

"Mister Popularity! Captain of the baseball team, student body president, homecoming king, prom king...ugh! It was enough to make me sick!"

"Okay, if I didn't know him, I'd agree with you. All those things combined are a bit much. But Mason was always a nice guy, so..." She shrugged. "It's just who he is, Scar. What's the big deal?"

Rolling her eyes, she was about to go off on a rant when their server returned with their food. With a muttered thanks, she opted to reach for her burger and take a huge bite instead.

And damn...as far as distractions went, this was the best one yet. It was almost enough for her to forget what they were talking about.

"You should probably get to know him before you get so judgy," Courtney said as she picked up her own burger. "I bet if you spent some time talking to him..."

"Oh, I know him, Court. Back in middle school we were

lab partners for a short time. He was semi-decent and kind of nice, but once high school hit, it was like he didn't even know me. So...I stand by my earlier opinion, thank you very much."

"Look, I get you have issues with people you think lead a privileged life...

"You have no idea."

Courtney gave her a hard stare before she continued. "However, sometimes you have to remember that looks can be deceiving and you have no idea what goes on behind closed doors."

Doing her best to appear bored, she reached for an onion ring. "And sometimes it's all exactly as it seemed. Sometimes shiny happy people are exactly that–shiny happy people with no substance."

"Well damn."

With a shrug, Scarlett took another bite of her burger and pushed all thoughts of Mason Bishop completely out of her mind.

**To preorder *In Case you Didn't Know*, click here!**

## ABOUT THE AUTHOR

Samantha Chase is a New York Times and USA Today bestseller of contemporary romance. She released her debut novel in 2011 and currently has more than forty titles under her belt! When she's not working on a new story, she spends her time reading romances, playing way too many games of Scrabble or Solitaire on Facebook, wearing a tiara while playing with her sassy pug Maylene...oh, and spending time with her husband of 25 years and their two sons in North Carolina.

Where to Find Me:
Website: www.chasing-romance.com

Sign up for my mailing list and get exclusive content and chances to win members-only prizes!
http://bit.ly/1jqdxPR

facebook.com/SamanthaChaseFanClub

twitter.com/SamanthaChase3

## ALSO BY SAMANTHA CHASE

**The Enchanted Bridal Series:**

The Wedding Season

Friday Night Brides

The Bridal Squad

Glam Squad & Groomsmen

**The Magnolia Sound Series**

Sunkissed Days

Remind Me

A Girl Like You

In Case You Didn't Know

**The Montgomery Brothers Series:**

Wait for Me

Trust in Me

Stay with Me

More of Me

Return to You

Meant for You

I'll Be There

Until There Was Us

Suddenly Mine

A Dash of Christmas

**The Shaughnessy Brothers Series:**

Made for Us

Love Walks In

Always My Girl

This is Our Song

Sky Full of Stars

Holiday Spice

Tangled Up in You

**Band on the Run Series:**

One More Kiss

One More Promise

One More Moment

**The Christmas Cottage Series:**

The Christmas Cottage

Ever After

**Silver Bell Falls Series:**

Christmas in Silver Bell Falls

Christmas On Pointe

A Very Married Christmas

A Christmas Rescue

## Life, Love & Babies Series:

The Baby Arrangement

Baby, Be Mine

Baby, I'm Yours

## Preston's Mill Series:

Roommating

Speed Dating

Complicating

## The Protectors Series:

Protecting His Best Friend's Sister

Protecting the Enemy

Protecting the Girl Next Door

Protecting the Movie Star

## 7 Brides for 7 Soldiers

Ford

Logan

## Standalone Novels

Jordan's Return

Catering to the CEO

In the Eye of the Storm

A Touch of Heaven